# DATING HAMLET

LISA FIEDLER

# DATING HAMLET
## Ophelia's Story

Henry Holt and Company
New York

Henry Holt and Company, LLC
*Publishers since 1866*
115 West 18th Street
New York, New York 10011
www.henryholt.com

Henry Holt is a registered trademark of Henry Holt and Company, LLC

Library of Congress Cataloging-in-Publication Data
Fiedler, Lisa.
Dating Hamlet: Ophelia's story / by Lisa Fiedler.
p.    cm.
Summary: In a story based on the Shakespeare play, Ophelia describes her relationship
with Hamlet, learns the truth about her own father, and recounts the complicated
events following the murder of Hamlet's father.
[1. Revenge—Fiction.    2. Murder—Fiction.    3. Princes—Fiction.]
I. Shakespeare, William 1564–1616. Hamlet.    II. Title.
PZ7.F457 Dat 2002    [Fic]—dc21       2002068902

ISBN 0-8050-7054-0 / First Edition—2002
Printed in the United States of America on acid-free paper. ∞
1  3  5  7  9  10  8  6  4  2

To the illustrious members of
Prose & Plenty—
Pamela Bramhall, Pamela Farley, and Barbara Mariconda

ॐ ॐ ॐ

I count myself in nothing else so happy
As in a soul remembering my good friends.

—William Shakespeare, *King Richard II*

## CHAPTER ONE

THE NIGHTS AT ELSINORE ARE LONGER THAN ANY-
where else. But I have never been anywhere else; I merely
imagine this to be true.

And this one is longer than most, a night without
slumber.

I am filled with such restlessness, as though I am being
taunted by the moon itself. I perspire, though it is more
cool than warm, and toss in my bed like one who is mad
with fever.

There is no help for it, and my thoughts settle on Hamlet.
Prince of Denmark.

Home now from school in Wittenberg, twice two
months, summoned hither with news of the tragedy. Before
then, I was forced to endure his absence, with only his
cherished missives to assure me of his devotion.

Since his return, we have whispered gentle promises and sworn upon our very souls that we, indeed, are meant to spend eternity in each other's arms. He is all known and unknown to me, a sweet secret, and I do revel in the study of him. He is a diamond in moonlight, glinting in facets of unimaginable number. He is water rippling in moonlight, he is moonlight itself.

I believe he hath stolen the smile of Apollo—and wears it to far greater effect. It warms me even in the memory of it.

Oh, and he is as brilliant as he is handsome, and he speaks to me in a voice that is at once rough and tender. We talk of past and future and all that comes between, and we speak of art and music and literature, for Hamlet does so love words.

Ah, words! Hamlet revels in them! He loves to tumble words over themselves, upending their meaning and playing on their sounds. When he speaks, I must listen with my understanding tipped at an angle that would make most others dizzy! 'Tis true—but only for the placing of one letter, do meanings slant and distort and become others— trust becomes tryst; friend, fiend—while one word's position among its fellows can make some sentence another. Hamlet hath shown me that a word is as good as a kiss, when, like a kiss, one knows how to bestow it.

And as brilliant and handsome as Hamlet is, he is even sweeter still. When no one watches, he presses his lips in careful kisses against my fingertips. Together, we talk of the sun and the stars and the earth, and of how we wish at times we were the only two who dwelled upon it. We speak of flowers, of their beauty and their meaning, and I present him with blossoms I have grown, or small bouquets, which he keeps, he tells me, 'neath his pillow.

He speaks of making me his wife, and I am told that the Queen finds favor in this.

But, alas, for near four months, Hamlet has dealt only in darkness. Since the death of his father, the King, my Prince has been . . . I can only name it melancholy, overcome with a most agonizing grief. He speaks little, and his eyes often gaze at something grim and far off that only Hamlet does see. Would that he could share his pain with me; would that I could ease his worried heart with a word, a touch, or even a silence of my own.

'Tis nearly morn, and sleep is distant, still; the creeping dread returns, and I am out of bed, pacing among the shadows.

Something strange is upon us, I know it, something I cannot name. Be it curse or blessing, I am not sure, but it comes for me, like some mystic messenger, and tugs at my sleeve. I dare not ignore it, for it calls.

Quietly, I dress, and quietly, I leave my room. "Anne will come," I tell myself. In the dawn stillness of the castle I make my way to the kitchens.

Anne is a servant's daughter, a servant herself; she rises early. We are friends, despite the great discrepancies of our birth. We are six-and-ten years now, but we have been as sisters 'most all of our lives. My mother, saints rest her, would bring us both to play beside the gentle brook that just beyond Elsinore runs; she cared not what Anne's station was, only that she could be a friend to me.

I believe I loved Anne instantly, for she made me laugh like no one else, save Laertes. It has been thus ever since.

Anne is the careful one. When I find her in the scullery and tell her my design, her eyes open fully, and her pretty mouth falls.

"No!" she gasps. "No, Lia!"

"Yes," I say. "Tell them I've summoned you to . . . assist me in washing my hair."

"Your hair has just been washed," she reminds me. "A mere four days past."

I lift my eyes to heaven. "Then tell them something else. But you must come."

Anne's chin trembles. "To the guard's platform?"

"That is what I said."

"But why?"

"I confess, I know not." I sit down on a stool and pick up an apple. "But I feel I must go. The moon wills it. Some secret knowing shudders inside me."

"Secret knowing, hah!" Anne, more herself now, snatches away the apple and returns it to its basket. "You go only in the hopes of finding the Prince there."

I eye a tray of meat pies. Anne slides them away with a snort.

"Why would Hamlet be about at this hour?" I challenge.

"I know not," says Anne. "It is only that everything you do these last months touches somehow on Hamlet. You sigh whene'er he walks past. It is no wonder that I should assume it is he you stalk at dawn."

"I do not wish to argue," I tell her, then add pleadingly, "You will join me?"

"I shall be whipped, mark it."

"You are never whipped. Let us go now."

After but a moment's pause, Anne says she will accompany me. I never doubted it. She sees to a simmering pot first, and then we make haste.

From the kitchen, through the cavernous hall, outdoors and up the moonlit stairs to the guard's watch. The air bites our faces; already my slippers are damp with dew.

Oh, I am awake and alive, even in the gloom! The vast stoniness of the walls is colorless but for their dusting of quartz. We climb toward the sky as it swirls above us. We are high, so high, where only men are allowed. This fills me with more than excitement. Anne says I was born to misbehave. Perhaps she is correct.

In the east, the sky is milky gray, not yet daylit.

Anne hears them first.

"Shhh," she hisses, grabbing my sleeve. I stop to listen.

The voices approaching are familiar. One in particular is that of Horatio—friend of Hamlet, schoolfellow at

Wittenberg, a guest at Elsinore for the funeral, but gone these many days.

Anne's eyes gleam with surprised joy. "Horatio hath returned?"

"Apparently."

Horatio is quite beauteous, built coarse and lean, with wide shoulders, tall as well. Anne is taken with him, verily. I've seen her look upon him as a starving man might look on bread.

She knows that Horatio, before his departure, did believe he loved me. But for all his beauty, Horatio was not for me. And to his great credit, Horatio quit his courtship when he learned of Hamlet's intentions in my regard. That, I always felt, spoke of the depth of their friendship.

From the guard's walk, I hear the officer Marcellus and Horatio as they greet the guard Barnardo. It is a moment before the dull-witted oaf notices that Marcellus has been joined by Horatio. "What, is Horatio there?" he inquires.

Horatio's golden voice ripples with his response. "A piece of him."

"Any piece is sufficient," Anne whispers to me with a grin.

I strain to hear them as they go on to speak of a visitation they expect this night.

Aha! Something *is* about! I knew as much; the moon told me. . . . Something dreaded is expected to arrive. The damp night crawls suddenly along my spine; I thirst for more, for more. . . .

Anne is cooing over Horatio's auburn hair. I hush her firmly. 'Tis not the time to admire a boy's locks, no matter how luxurious they may be.

They continue their discourse, and now I learn from Marcellus that which they fear. The words reach me as though on a wisp of smoke; he foretells the coming of an apparition.

*An apparition!* The very breath catches in my throat.

"What?" begs Anne, who did not hear. "What causes you to tremble, Lia? They speak in such shrouded voices."

Shrouded, yes. Shrouded like death itself, which, they say, has walked this very watch among them. I take a step to reveal my presence, but Anne pulls me back. She is right, of course. I do not belong here. Yet I am fascinated.

"Pray tell," Anne whispers. "On what subject do they argue?"

"The guards have seen a ghost . . ." I explain, then cover her mouth to muffle the scream. "Twice. On this very spot, at this very hour, two nights now. Marcellus has brought Horatio to prove them true, to confirm their vision, though Horatio is convinced the ghost does not exist."

"His eyes are like topaz, are they not?" Anne intrudes in dreamy tones.

"Anne! Hush! You may be lovesick later. For the moment, please, be still and listen." I draw a breath and go on. "If it comes, tonight they will rely upon Horatio to speak to it."

"It?"

"The apparition!"

Anne crosses herself mightily. I am not sure if 'tis the thought of an apparition or the thought of her beloved engaging one in conversation that distresses her more. For good measure, I cross myself as well.

Now Marcellus cries out for silence. At this, I fear I am found. But he notices me not at all.

Marcellus points at something. In a tone most disbelieving, Barnardo remarks that it is the same figure like the King that's dead.

The King that's dead! This revelation pierces me like a dagger, but slowly, as though the blade were blunt. The King that's dead . . . my Hamlet's father?

I peer round the parapet behind which we've secluded ourselves and stare fiercely at what is at first vaporous emptiness but now becomes a figure, a specter turned out for battle.

A man.

The King.

The deceased King, to be precise! My heart leaps, though whether with joy or terror 'tis hard to say.

Anne is no help. She faints dead away.

Marcellus demands that Horatio speak to the ghost.

"What art thou?" comes the echo of brave Horatio's voice. "By heaven I charge thee, speak!"

I am not surprised that the ghost . . . the King . . . the King's ghost . . . says naught. His Highness is no doubt unused to being ordered so.

"It is offended," Marcellus observes.

Well, of course it is offended! He is the King, even in death—or half-death, or after death, or whatsoever this state be called.

Surely it is Hamlet the apparition seeks; surely someone should offer to fetch the Prince! But men know only orders. I would speak to that ghost myself, did I not fear the guards, in their agitated state, might react badly and run me through. Besides, it is too late. I gaze in disgust as the apparition withdraws, vanishes.

"How now, Horatio?" says Barnardo, a bit smugly. "You tremble and look pale. Is not this something more than fantasy?"

I strain to hear more—Horatio, employing mayhap some intuition of his own, suggests that a visitation such as this bodes strange eruption to our state.

Now Horatio and the others turn their talk to war, to disputes with one called Fortinbras, and to that most mindless masculine obsession, vengeance.

I nudge Anne with my toe; she stirs, and I smile down at her.

"Ah. You've not died. That is good."

Her first thought: "Horatio—is he well?"

"Quite," I inform her, "for one who's just encountered the spirit of the King. And, I might add, behaved poorly."

Anne, dear Anne, just blinks.

But before I can go on, I am halted by more excited voices from the platform. Anne remains where she is—sprawled on the stones—but I lean farther around the wall, so I might see better this time.

The ghost has returned! This time I am unafraid and prepare to speak. I've a million inquiries I would make of it. But Horatio speaks ere I even open my mouth. True to his gender, the fool accosts the noble spirit with—of all things—politics!

Shame on Horatio! When one meets a ghost, one should query on heaven and hell, on the meaning of life, on any number of the most divine obscurities—but this *boy* seeks military advantage?

Marcellus suggests to strike it! To my great shock, Horatio encourages the violence!

Unable to control myself, I gasp.

Horatio makes but the slightest start at my sound, and I see him tilt his ear in my direction. Again, my breath holds in my throat. And now he makes a near-indiscernible glance—away from the spirit, toward my hiding place. And *now* . . . a smile? Yes, methinks I saw the man smile!

Returning his attention—and a countenance less amused—to the dead King, Horatio and his fellow soldiers make to attack it. But before they strike, there comes the sound of crowing, and the ghost into the coming daylight fades, first to vapor, then to absence. Had I not seen it with mine own eyes, I'd not believe it. But it is so.

Horatio and Marcellus remark on't; Barnardo, fiddling with his dagger, has nothing to offer.

'Tis my opinion that the ghost simply tired of them and their inappropriate behavior. I listen unseen as they plan to report the happening to Hamlet. But I shall beat them to it. God save me, I shall go directly to Hamlet.

"My lady . . . a word."

I turn to find Horatio, separate from his companions now, standing behind me.

Anne is aglaze and speechless. I am mostly angered with myself for being caught.

"Horatio! Why, welcome once again to Elsinore, my lord."

"I thank you, m'lady. But I would know, wherefore thou art about at this late hour?" His demand is softened by the warmth in his eyes.

"It is not late, sir," I tell him. "It is early."

"The world is dark."

"It grows lighter as we watch," I tell him, with a lift of my chin toward the east, where the night holds hands with morning. "Unless it is to its disposition you refer, then, yea, sir, the world is surely dark."

Horatio lowers one eyebrow at me. "How much have you heard?"

"Enough."

"Enough?"

"Enough to draw the same baffling conclusions as thee."

"Nothing, my lady, of this world or any other, does

baffle me so much as you." A smile twitches at the corners of his mouth, and he leans close to me. "How go things with Hamlet? He was most despondent when last I saw him. I expect he is not overly attentive to thee in such a cloudy condition. I, on the other hand . . ."

Men! Can they not think on anything but conquest, of one sort or another? I interrupt him.

"Some ladies find a melancholy beau appealing."

"Some ladies?"

"Aye."

"Pray tell, is the fair Ophelia one of those ladies?"

"We have at length discussed this, Horatio, and my decision is as ever."

Horatio shrugs and smiles. "One cannot blame a man for trying."

"Hear me, Horatio. I love Hamlet. And I know you, like a brother, love him too. You would not dream to lure me from him."

Horatio sighs. "Would that I could. . . ." ('Tis muttered.)

I ignore it. Anne, at last, sees fit to remove herself from the floor. I assist her in dusting the filth from her skirts, then turn back to Horatio.

"Now . . . what shall we?"

"We?"

"Yes, we. You've devised to tell Hamlet of this ghostly encounter, and I would play a part in it."

"Oh, no . . ." Now his hand is firm upon my shoulder.

"I shall speak to Hamlet. You will hold thy tongue. Speak not of what you've witnessed."

"To none but Hamlet."

"Nay, to Hamlet least of all." He grins again. "For to do that, thou wouldst need admit to being here."

He doth have a point. I frown. "Think you that Hamlet would be angered to know I was here?"

"Angered?" Horatio laughs gustily. "At you? No, dear lady, I doubt he would even know how to be angered with thee. My worry is for my own skin, should the Prince learn that his love hath been about at daybreak, unchaperoned, in my company. He would go mad!"

With that, my erstwhile suitor guides Anne and myself down the stairs. I pay no attention to his laughter, for I am thinking too intently on his words. Hamlet has never seemed to me the jealous sort. Has he communicated otherwise to Horatio? 'Tis possible.

There is also the half-chance that my lord will find the boldness of my actions cause for concern.

But, oh, to be the one to reveal that his father's spirit wakes. . . .

Confusion boils in me. To tell. Or not to tell?

Hah! Confusion is short-lived.

*For I, Ophelia, am not one to suffer the plague of indecison.*
*I will act! And tell my love of this night's most ghostly vision.*

## CHAPTER TWO

HAMLET DOES NOT SLEEP. HE SITS AND STARES AS A chill invades his chamber through the open window. He sits close by it, breathing deep of the cold, coming day.

"My lord?"

I expect him to whirl, astounded, and yet he makes only a slow turn of his head to face me.

"My lord, you are awake."

"I am."

Oh, how his voice does trouble me. What would I give to abandon this grim mission and instead spend sunrise in his arms?

"My lord, I have news. I have been . . . out."

"I have been out myself, my lady. Out of sorts, surely. Out of . . ."

"Soft, my lord . . . forgive me, but I must say what I must say. I have been out . . . on the guard's platform."

"The guard's platform, lady? Did you seek to be of some assistance to the soldiers?"

(Little does he know how desperately they required it!)

"No, my lord. I went on an inkling. I believed something was to be seen there."

Hamlet rises now, makes his way toward me, and stands close. I feel his breath; his chest comes even with my forehead.

"And were you correct?" He whispers this, his thumb beneath my chin, lifting.

"I was, sir."

There is a kiss waiting. I reach for it, eyes closed, and rise on tiptoe. My Hamlet meets me, lips to lips, tenderly and possessed of a calm satisfaction I've not felt from him in weeks. It nearly does me in. The kiss lasts moments, hours, days. It is a second at most, but enough.

"Tell me."

"I saw . . . the King."

His muscles go taut, rigid with hatred. "Claudius was on the guard's watch?"

"No."

"But Claudius is King."

"Aye, my lord, and Denmark be the worse for it."

This earns a smile, a sweeter kiss. "I do love thee, Ophelia."

"And I thee, my lord."

"But . . ."

Nay, not but! I brace myself. "My lord?"

"I am sorry."

"Sorry?"

"For I am torn, my lady, at the very seams of my being. On the one side, I am teeming with such indescribable happiness, the total cause of which is that I lay mine eyes on you!"

"This sounds not like something for which one should apologize."

"Nay, love, but it is not the happiness in my heart for which I beg pardon. It is the other side, the side which harbors a sadness so sharp it slices me to the core. I despise life, even as I adore it. I am split, you see, catapulted to heaven by my love for you, and dashed to hell with the thought of enduring life in such a world as this."

"I am content with the half that loves me," I assure him.

"Grateful am I that you say so, lady, but, God, O God, can it be fair?" His torment sends him pacing, wide, weary strides as heavy as his thoughts. "Is it fair I ask you love me when I love nothing in my sight save you?"

"You never asked, Hamlet. I love you of my own accord."

And now, of a sudden, I find myself wrapped in his arms, pulled fast against him. He smells manly, of clean linen, and new leather, and fire—holding me tight for long, long minutes, while his chest heaves with great sobs.

When again he speaks, his voice is gently gruff. "You will not feel abandoned, then? You will understand that the part of myself where I keep your love is safe and separate from the part so riddled with despair?"

"I understand, dear Hamlet."

He laughs at this, then steadies himself with a breath. "Now, then, love. Pray, what did you see on the platform?"

"A ghost."

Hamlet steps backward and regards me with narrow eyes. "Seek you to make me laugh some more?"

"No. There is nothing humorous in this, sir. I saw a ghost. The ghost of our late King. Your father's spirit, Hamlet! I swear by Saint James' sandal, it is so. I saw it."

There is something in his eyes now—some stony hesitation that is not quite disbelief. He studies me, and I meet his gaze. "I grant it is difficult to take for truth, but you must, good Hamlet. Do not doubt it."

"You do not doubt it, lady, I shall." He is already three strides toward the door, but I call him back.

"Not now. 'Tis nearly full light, and he has gone. But he will return. The same instinct that sent me out this night tells me so. Something is sorely unsettled if such a noble spirit as your father's cannot rest."

Hamlet drops to a seat, one hand rakes his lovely hair, and his face is filled with hope and horror. "What could be so wicked that could drag a man from death?"

"I believe he will tell you."

He thinks on this, his eyes shining. "Who else saw?"

"The guard Barnardo. Marcellus. And Horatio."

"Horatio. My trusted friend. He is here? And saw the spirit. Yet he has not come to tell me."

"He plans to, my lord. I suspect he delays only so as not to disturb your sleep."

"Sleep . . . ," says Hamlet. "I barely remember the state."

"Aye, sir. I understand."

"Did Horatio or the others speak to the ghost?"

"Horatio attempted but failed miserably. I thought to try but feared the men would disapprove. I wanted to tell the spirit of your enduring devotion, your deep sadness, and your love. Horatio discovered me and advised that I keep silent, as it is unseemly for me to be roaming the castle at dawn."

"I am sure you had good reason for your wandering."

"I did, my lord. The moon beckoned me."

Hamlet sighs. "I am familiar with that call."

"Horatio was concerned that you might be troubled by even my accidental nearness to him." I pause, then venture boldly: "Are you, my lord?"

"Do you ask if I am jealous, love?"

I lift one shoulder in a shrug. "Yes, I suppose I do."

Again, he gives me the gift of his laughter. "You are as honest as you are lovely," he tells me. "And so I will be honest with thee. Aye, I am desperately jealous of Horatio. And Marcellus, and Barnardo, and the groom who tends to your mare, and the servant who sets your plate before you, and the one who clears it away. In short, my lady, I am jealous of any man who has even the briefest opportunity to look upon you!"

I cannot suppress a scowl. "I thought you trusted me!"

"I do trust you, sweet Ophelia. It is the entire male gender which I mistrust. My greatest fear is that one day a better man than I will come along and steal you away."

"There is no better man than you," I assure him, tingling at the flattery. "But as I do not wish to be scolded by Horatio when he brings this news, please do not let on that I have beat him to it."

"I swear it." He kisses me once more, and there is starlight in it. "You must go."

"I wish you sleep, sweet Hamlet."

"And I wish you the same. Good night, Ophelia."

"Good night."

Another kiss, and I am gone.

❦ ❦ ❦

I dress.

A day gown, the color of the moon, embroidered at the cuffs with silver-pink roses. Customarily, 'tis Anne who dresses me, but, wanting to miss nothing, I have sent her ahead for a most significant purpose. Now I am at the mercy of the Queen's eldest attendant. I urge her to make haste, impatient with her for she is meticulous and precise—every fastening fixed, every wrinkle smoothed. When

Anne assists me in the burdensome task of getting dressed, we hurry so that 'tis a wonder I manage to leave my chamber with my ankles concealed.

I am wanted in the audience chamber with the rest of the courtiers. The new King Claudius, uncle to Hamlet and now stepfather as well, has summoned one and all. Anne, at this very moment, will be pressing herself against the railing of the gallery, listening for news to report to me. Were I not so interested in two of the points at issue, I would not e'en attend.

Oh, what an ugly affair it is, and yet all of them smile and smile, toasting the circumstance as if 'twere blessed. I loathe it, and fear it. This is how it goes:

Our King Hamlet died suddenly, not four months past. The Queen, his widow, my Hamlet's beloved mother, did mourn him greatly at first.

And yet, such agony did not last.

Too soon the sobbing ceased, too sudden were made the plans to marry. Queen Gertrude was to become wife to the brother of her husband. I imagined her cheeks still damp with tears of mourning whilst her newlywed King splattered his unjust kisses upon them.

In truth, it all disgusted me. Disgusts me still.

And to see the pained expression on Hamlet's face as the vows were spoken. That was the start of his melancholy mood—as if the loss of his father were not enough! It is even sickening to say it—his uncle now his father, his mother now his aunt. It is nothing less than evil, nothing less than sin.

It is a celebration of this sin to which I hurry now. I will take no pleasure in it, I go only because my father, Polonius, wills it so.

My father . . . Shall I even begin?

Some find him quite entertaining, a comical sort, who revels in the sound of his own voice, regardless whether there be matter in his words. I have long ago come to understand that my father does not love me. It is not for anything I've done or not done. Love is an emotion for which he has no use. He boasts of my brother, a student, a soldier, a son—but I am a daughter, a useless burden; he will see to my marriage and forget me.

But my mother loved me dearly and my brother, Laertes, as well.

He is very like our mother, Laertes is. Kind and beautiful and wise. Laertes loves me—I know this to be true. He is as no brother ever was—devoted, concerned, sometimes a nuisance, but always a dear friend. He worries after me, which I have never quite understood but always liked.

Laertes used to fret over such things as my falling from horses and developing rashes from too close contact with my flowers (which he teasingly calls weeds). His worry has taken a new turn of late—and Hamlet, having made his affection for me known, is at the root of it. Laertes' worry increases with the blossoming of my womanly figure. It is funny, and he is dear.

Laertes will speak to the King today, to learn whether he be permitted to return to France. I will ache for his absence but eagerly will await his return and the magnificent tales it will bring.

Yes, Laertes will speak to the King . . . and Horatio to the Prince. I heard him bid Marcellus join him in telling Hamlet what he hath witnessed on the watch; they will do so once the King's gathering has dispersed.

In the audience chamber, all is glad and raucous. I slip in, unnoticed by all but Hamlet, who stays to himself, at a short but purposeful distance. His gaze rests on me for a long moment, and there is the memory of our last kiss in it.

I fix my eyes upon the King, who, from his high perch upon his brother's throne, is a disquieting sight. His garments are of fine silk, his fingers are crowded with jeweled rings, heavy and glinting in the heavenly streamers of sunlight which inappropriately bathe him and his stolen Queen.

The Queen! Oh, how I once loved her. When married to King Hamlet, she was a proud and gentle presence. In truth, I thought Gertrude much like my own mother—a beauty, with playful spirit and fertile mind. But now I see she has misplaced her loveliness. She has the same bright-cobalt eyes as my Hamlet, and her smiling lips are petal-toned, also like his. But to me, today, she is cold and colorless—even as she doth blush warmly beneath her husband's touch.

I arrive in time to hear the repugnant King inform good Hamlet that he shall not be permitted to return to school.

Oh, they deny him to go to Wittenberg! I all but shatter into joyful fragments of myself. Hamlet stays! But guilt swiftly trespasses upon this most selfish gladness, as my thoughts lean toward Hamlet's desires.

Would he be lighter at Wittenberg, away from the ostentatious affection of his mother for her King? Does he long to be away, to free himself from the waking nightmare of this place?

I turn to him, and I fear I will see disappointment in his eyes. But it is in this instant that Hamlet turns to me, and, in the space of a heartbeat . . . he smiles.

He is pleased to remain! No doubt, I am beyond pleased to have him do so. And then dear Hamlet, my boyish Prince, surprises me with a sudden wink. It is flirtation, part, but something more.

A secret. A promise.

A prayer.

 తి తి తి

Anne has been hiding in the gallery. When the assemblage disperses, I hurry to meet her. We seclude ourselves there to listen as Horatio reports to Hamlet.

Hamlet is alone, awaiting the arrival of his friends. I am

curious to hear if Horatio will be full true in his testimony. Will he confess his poor manners, his aggressive stance in the King's presence? Or will he shave away the more prickly whiskers of the story to show himself smooth to judgment's touch?

Now Hamlet's solitude is stolen by the sound of footsteps as Horatio, Marcellus, and Barnardo enter. Barnardo looks as though he has already forgotten why he's come. 'Tis true what Hamlet says of him: he is not the pointiest arrow in the quiver!

Hamlet and Horatio embrace. Now I shall learn how gifted a player is Hamlet.

Talk is small at first; then Hamlet, eager to get on with it, offers an inroad, confiding to Horatio, "My father— methinks I see my father."

"Where, my lord?"

"In my mind's eye, Horatio . . ."

The subject has surfaced. Now it is for Horatio, and he does not disappoint.

"My lord, I think I saw him yesternight."

Hamlet's expression is properly confused. "Saw who?"

"My lord," says Horatio, "the King, your father."

"The King, my father?"

Horatio holds up his hand, and asks for Hamlet's indulgence of what will surely be a tale beyond belief. I lean so far o'er the balcony that Anne must clutch my skirt to keep me from toppling.

Horatio gives his testimony—the guards, the watch, the approximate time. He describes the ghost and relays that he was armed. He makes no mention of his commanding tone, nor does he admit his inclination to strike the apparition with his sword. It is for this reason I regret that men record history; they include only the details which reflect well upon themselves.

"'Tis very strange," says Hamlet, as if he's been told nothing of it before; he blinks and shakes his head in consternation. (I almost believe his amazement myself!)

"I will watch tonight," Hamlet whispers. "Perchance 'twill walk again."

Before they depart, Hamlet implores them to keep their silence. He says he will visit them upon the platform 'twixt eleven and twelve.

(Will he visit me at ten? He is surely welcome.)

When they have gone, Anne hurries away that she might cross paths with Horatio in the hall. Hamlet lifts his divine eyes to mine in the gallery.

"My father's spirit—in arms! All is not well. I doubt some foul play. Would the night were come. . . ."

(Aye, I am thinking, in particular the hour of ten!)

I wave to him a kiss from my fingertips, and he is off. Then Anne's voice is calling me from the hall, telling me I must to my father's quarters.

I have almost forgotten—my dear Laertes is to depart for France.

A storm does rage within me.

It is not just rain in my soul which pours from the cloud-swept emotion of Laertes' bittersweet farewell; there is also a rumbling thunder that echoes after the lightning of my father's harsh command. He has decreed that I am not to talk to the Lord Hamlet.

I repeat his bruising declaration to Anne. We are alone in my room, where I have thrown myself upon the pallet, and my tears spill freely, my fury overrun only by a deep, deep yearning to share this with my mother.

"He prohibits you even *speak* to Hamlet?" Anne is stunned. "He cannot mean that!"

"Oh, by the devil's long tail, he means it! While to my brother he gives advice . . . and gives, and *gives* advice . . . of a most trivial nature. 'Buy costly clothes. Dress well, keep your thoughts to yourself, resist the urge to borrow or lend a coin!' This is what he tells his son—'To thine own self be true.'"

Anne frowns. "How may one be true to oneself when one is expected to follow these many lofty and particular directives of another?"

"You see? My father is a fool, and a cruel-hearted one at that. For from his daugher he demands the very opposite—that I deny who I am, by forsaking the love that defines me."

Anne is quiet a moment. "Will you?"

"Will I? Aye, a will have I. And a most solid one, you mark it. I will what I will."

Anne rolls her eyes. "You speak now like Hamlet," she laments with a sigh. "I am lost. You've blown in here as on a bitter breeze to announce your father forbids you love your love. That I understand. But, marry, much is left unsaid."

"What else would you know?"

"Well, to begin," says Anne, "I would know what Laertes said to thee upon his leave."

I expel a long, windy breath. "He expressed most brotherly concerns."

"Touching Hamlet?"

"Aye, and touching Hamlet is most certainly not allowed."

"Lia!" Anne blushes, then shakes her head. "So Laertes' perception reflects your father's? He too would have you be scarce with the Prince?"

"Aye. He urged me think on Hamlet's attention as a condition not permanent. Sweet, but not lasting. I tell you, Anne, it was all I had to keep from breaking into laughter when talked he of a growing body as—believe you this?—a '*temple.*'"

"He did not!" Anne bursts into giggles.

"Aye," I say, giggling myself. "He did."

I move toward the collection of pots beside my window and absently examine a withering fennel plant which grows there. "He spoke of buds and blossoms, and how the cankerworm might be their ruin! His point, of course, had naught to do with botany but with chastity. Suffice it to say that my brother took great pains to suggest I protect my virtue from Hamlet's advances. He bid me not be gullible to Hamlet's pleading."

"Does Hamlet plead?"

"Well . . . I would not call it *pleading*, but he does propose, and coax, and both he does convincingly. Laertes warned that I might lose my heart, or—hear this one, Anne—my '*chaste treasure.*'"

"Hah!" Annes shakes her head. "Whilst he goes off to France to enjoy himself treasure-hunting among the women there!"

I sigh. "True. But I care not how my brother tends his garden, if you get my meaning. That is his business. As Hamlet is mine."

"And what," Anne whispers, "do you intend with regard to the matter of such tending?" She pauses to summon boldness, then inquires, "Would you give yourself to Hamlet soon?"

"That is a good question," I answer with a shrug. "I do not think so. I do love him. And I must allow that I have faith in Laertes, despite his silly speeches, for he does hold my best interests in his heart. But know you this, Anne, whatever I do *not* do with Hamlet I do *not* not do because I am ordered against doing it; but because *I* do choose not to do it!"

Anne takes a moment to translate. "Will Hamlet choose the same?"

"My choice will leave him none. But I sense that he will be most generously patient."

Anne smiles. "The moon's told you?"

"Aye."

"You amaze me, Lia, God's truth, you do."

I examine the plantings. "Did you know that lore links the fragrant fennel to flattery and deceit?"

"Aye, you've told me."

I pull a lifeless leaf from the stalk, then, crumbling it between my fingers, I sigh and move from the ledge to my worktable. It holds several cuttings, a scattering of roots, herbs, and a small book—my lady mother's journal—containing notes on how to combine them. My father was unaware that she possessed the remarkable ability to read and write, or that she taught me to do the same. I turn to a page marked with a silk ribbon. "See here, Anne. 'Tis the recipe for a fragrance beloved by my dear mother—a scented oil she mixed for herself, one I well recall."

"As do I," says Anne wistfully. "Your mama always smelled so lovely."

"Aye." I run my finger down the list of ingredients, and remember how, as a child, I was allowed to tip the silver flask that held the perfume and use my tiny forefinger to apply it to her pulse. Following her death, the flask came to me—alas, empty but for a single drop, which I saved until the night of Hamlet's first kiss.

"I have oft wondered," says Anne gently, "why you have never mixed the fragrance for thyself."

"I have thought to, many times," I confess. "But scent is a powerful reminder; I fear 'twould only remind me how very much I miss her. In addition, I would tell you that on the one occasion when I did wear the scent in Hamlet's company he found it most sultry and irresistible." I slant a grin at her. "I see no reason to tempt the poor boy more than he already is!"

Anne laughs.

"There is another reason," I confess. "Along with the recipe came a warning. My mother, in her graceful hand, did pen as well a caveat, cautioning that, but for one ingredient, through the magic of alchemy, her benign fragrance would become a *poison*. A poison that is not entirely a poison but a miraculous concoction, *approaching* poison, which only may become a poison when he who's consumed it is left untreated by its antidote for a certain span of time."

Anne gasps. "Honest?"

"According to my mother's records, the root of one flower, the stalk of a second, and the petal of yet another—crushed and added to the oil derived of a fourth—brings about the perfume. However, this perfume is the beginning of a venom that wants only a fifth flower to complete its evil. When properly administered, it shall induce a sleep so full, so genuine, that even the coroner himself would believe it death."

"But sleep looks naught like death," Anne reasons.

"This medicine is cunning," I assure her, "for it brings with its counterfeit sleep a tightening of the lung, a chilling of the flesh, and an ashen tint to the skin. Even the heart slows to a mere whisper of its own beat, but beat, good friend, it does. The condition is not immediately fatal. The sleep grows slowly deeper toward doom. If the cure comes in time, death does not take hold."

"Thank heaven there is an antidote," remarks Anne.

I neglect to mention that, since my mother, to the best of my knowledge, never actually brewed the antidote (or, for that matter, the poison), the exactitude of its proficiency is not entirely guaranteed, the information being gleaned from legend, not practice. I am also grateful that she does not question the indistinctness of the directive "a certain span of time." I know only that there is a span during which the poison remains benign. I know not precisely what that span may be.

"Intriguing," breathes Anne.

"Most intriguing," I agree. But, as I see no immediate use for such a worthy potion, I have not tried it yet.

I stir a calming physic until it bubbles, then drink it down. That done, I lie down upon my pallet so Anne can comb my hair. My thoughts return to my brother's admonition.

"Laertes thinks the Prince a danger, but for me, Lord Hamlet is the least fearful presence in this castle."

"What do you mean?"

"There is something dangerous here of late, and the very earth shifts beneath me. I am afraid that, to be honest to myself, as my own father advised his male child be, I must be false to others." I smile up at Anne. "But never to you, dear friend."

"Nor I to you. Never."

My storm subsides, and I close my eyes, to drift, to dream.

# CHAPTER THREE

I AWAKE, HOURS LATER, TO A GENTLE KNOCK UPON my chamber door. The moon, swollen with secrets, is at my window. It is the hour of ten.

I open the door to Hamlet. "How now, my lord?"

He shrugs. "I am nervous."

"That is to be expected."

He steps within. "Shall we share an hour, then, during which I may forget the strange event that is to come?"

"Aye."

"Then let's begin with this." From his neck he removes a glistening chain on which swings a bejeweled pendant; he lowers it over my head. The heavy charm rests beneath the hollow of my throat. "For thee, love. A token of my most genuine affection."

"It is lovely."

"It was," he says in a voice like silk, "though in this new location its wearer does surely outshine it." He leans down to place a chaste kiss on the bridge of my nose.

"I thank you, my lord."

"Now . . ." He motions to the plants along my window. "Tell me of your flowers. Do you find among them any new remedy, or property, or potion? Since my last visit— remember, when you bid me close my eyes, then challenged me to name each blossom by its scent?—what earthy secrets have they told you? What powdered petals have you mixed, and, pray, did they ignite, or smolder, or simply yield a more divine fragrance, similiar perhaps to the sweet- ness I oft taste in your breath before we kiss?"

I fold my arms and frown at him. "You tease me!"

"Ah! Then we are even!" Laughing, he catches me and spins me round. "The very sight of you teases me, Ophelia, and you well know it."

"I know it, but cannot help it, my Lord." He tickles me now and I cry out in delight. "'Tis not my fault you are but a weak, weak man!"

"I am not weak, Ophelia," says Hamlet, with a playful growl, "I am in love!"

"Oh, I do surely prefer that to weakness."

Here, he lowers me to the bed and fixes his eyes to mine. "Strange, how love that makes us weak does make us strong."

The bedclothes rustle beneath me, and there is only the sound of Hamlet's breathing as we embrace.

I should stop him. . . . Soft, not yet . . . *some more. Not all, but more.*

"I am less anxious than before . . . ," he begins, through a kiss.

"I disagree, my lord, to me you seem as anxious as ever, mayhap more."

He nips at my chin. "You do not let me finish."

"You may count on that, sir."

"Nymph!" Soundless laughter ripples in his belly against my own. "You are quick with words, you snap them at me like a whip."

"You taught me well."

"Would that I hadn't, else now I might succeed at getting one in edgewise."

"I shall leave *that* one alone," I whisper, nuzzling his cheek. "It is far too easy!"

"I mean only that tonight I suffer no anxiety over the chance your brother will discover us. He would murderously defend your honor."

"Must I remind you, Lord Hamlet, that to date my honor remains intact?"

"I need no reminder," he snarls, eyes dancing. "'Tis a fact well known to me!"

We stop speaking and continue our delicate exploration. Hamlet is everywhere warm and strong, and my palms seek, recalling every chiseled muscle of his arms and chest and back. His hands remember my curves as well, and move as though they long for what's familiar. And more for what is not.

When I bid him stop, he does not argue. Instead, he sits up and leans upon the wall. I snuggle close, my back against his chest, his arm about my waist.

"Tell me what you are thinking," I say, in but a dusting of my voice.

"Someday man will harvest lightning from the heavens!"

"Steal it from the gods, you mean?"

"Nay, he will bargain for it. He will dazzle the immortals with some knowledge of which you and I cannot yet even dream. He will earn the lightning, and the gods will give it gladly."

Oh, 'tis marvelous that my Hamlet thinks in such colors.

"What will man do with it?"

"He will turn night to day! And, of even greater import, he will have the means to keep himself warm when his lady says, 'Enough.'"

I roll my eyes and pinch him. "It is a magical thought."

"It is only magical at this time, in this place. In future, I believe, 'twill happen."

"Then speak to me of something sooner, something nearer to this realm."

"Oh, well, that is simple." He places his lips to linger at my ear. "I shall have you."

"Aye, when we are wed."

"Nay, before that."

I turn to him, biting back a smile, and raise my brows in warning. "Careful . . ."

"Oh, I will be, when the time comes."

I return his saucy grin. "You are bold, sir, and incorrect."

He chuckles in reply. "I am bold, lady, but as to incorrect, well, only time will tell of that. For I fear, if I do not have you soon, I surely will go mad!"

And now another knock. Marcellus, come to bid him take his leave. I remove myself from his arms, and Hamlet is to the door in three broad steps.

"Return here," I tell him, "as soon as 'tis done."

"I will be late."

"I will not mind."

"Done, then." He waves me a kiss. "God give you a good night."

"He already has, my lord."

I listen until the hollow sound of his footsteps no longer can be heard. Then I rise and make to my pots of herbs and flowers, where I collect several blooms, some leaves, a stem or two, then petals again.

Mayhap Hamlet's jest was not so far off the mark. Alchemy, after all, is close akin to love—it is all in the blending! Until we learn to tempt the lightning from the sky, we shall have to rely on what magic springs from earth.

So I begin, by rubbing one satiny petal between my fingers. Sooner or later, I am certain, something is bound to ignite!

ლ ლ ლ

"There is much to be told!"

These are the words that awaken me. Hamlet's words,

uttered in a whisper which carries the urgency of a shout. It is close to dawn; the cold has come in with him, clinging to his face and hands and hair.

"What, my lord?" I sit up, arranging the flannel sleeping gown closely about me against the chill he brings. "Hast thou seen thy father's spirit?"

"Aye, lady, and we have spoken."

"Tell me! Tell all."

"I shall." He draws a low stool near to the fire and sits upon it.

Backlit there in dancing golden hues, his shadow shuddering on the hearth before him, my Hamlet looks himself a ghost. I rise from the bed and approach him, dragging a small bench for my seat.

Hamlet opens his mouth to speak, but words spring first to my own lips. "Was he well? Spoke he of angels on high, or of fiends in fiery depths? Oh, and does he continue to feel, to taste, to hunger and thirst? For I have always wondered that. And what of purgatory? God's eyes, I have so long worried if there is, in fact, such a place. Does he miss you, Hamlet? Does he pine for Gertrude? And what of—"

"Ophelia . . ."

"My lord?"

"Hush."

His eyes dance upon me, shining with kind, impatient humor.

"Oh! I am sorry, my lord. It is only that I ache to know!"

"That is apparent, love. But if you would stop aching aloud, I may enlighten you."

"Yes, yes, my lord. Please, do."

"He came. I was nearly paralyzed at first, though with fear or with wonderment, I know not. My heart, Ophelia, at the sight of him, did pound as though I had swallowed thunder. He was armed."

"I remember."

"He beckoned me, and, naturally, I followed."

"Naturally, my lord? I would think, given his present circumstance, it was a most unnatural occurrence."

"All right, then. Unnaturally, I followed. . . ."

"But, then, he is your father, and so . . ."

"Ophelia . . ."

"Aye?"

A frown is his reply.

"I am sorry."

"So you have said."

"Go on."

He rises from the stool and goes to the window. "He did not have long to speak, for the hour of his banishment drew nigh." He slides a look my way. "Most fortunately for him, his audience did not interrupt."

I roll my eyes and press my lips together firmly.

"Such a wretched truth did he impart, love. The King was murdered."

"Nay!"

"Murdered! Poison, administered while the good King slept."

"Then he made no confession?"

"He did not. He took with him the imperfections of his humanity, and now he does pay dearly for them. But there is more, there is worse. . . ."

My mouth is dry, my hands are shaking. "Naught could be worse. . . ."

"He was murdered at the hand of his own brother!"

"Claudius!" A shriek releases itself from my throat like a demon escaping hell.

"Aye." Hamlet's eyes darken and he grinds the name through his teeth. "Claudius."

I bound to my feet, grasping the first article within my reach—a pot of daisies in poor health—which I smash to the floor. "Damn his soul to hell! Damn him!" I reach for something else—a book—and fling it against the wall. "Damn his eyes, and his vile heart, and his nose, and each one of his gnarled teeth, and damn every last follicle of hair on his body!"

"That is a most thorough damning, love," says Hamlet calmly.

"Oh, oh . . . ," I sputter. "Now *you* hush."

His brows arc upward, fast. He watches as I hunt down my slippers and step into them.

"What need is there for shoes?"

"I am off to Claudius's chamber." I push Hamlet aside

and search the shelf at my window until I find the wooden crucible used earlier this night.

"What have you?"

"Poison."

"Did you say *poison*, lady?"

"Well, presently, 'tis perfume, but the addition of a single element shall turn it lethal."

Hamlet blinks at me as I search my garden for the fatal component.

"Do not look at me so, Highness, for the fault of it is yours!"

*"Mine?"* Hamlet plants his hands on his hips and meets me in two great strides. "Forgive me, dear lady, but I did pass this night consorting with a ghost, with whom I discussed villainy and vengeance; I recall no discourse on venom with thee. And yet you say I bid you mix a poison."

"Not precisely, my lord. But you did speak to me of flowery secrets, and things igniting." I wring my hands a moment, then stop myself. I stand taller and meet his gaze. "Claudius took your father's life with poison."

"So you wish to punish him in kind?"

"Don't you?"

He stares at me, then mutters 'neath his breath, "Talk about things igniting."

I put down the crucible, which still contains mere fragrance, and give him an impatient sigh. "I abhor the thought of it, but 'tis the only course—or so the dull-witted, war-mongering *men* of this earth would have thee believe. Claudius laid himself open to retaliation the moment he did take his brother's life."

Hamlet draws me near to him. "Forgive me, love, I am confused. You denounce revenge e'en as you hand me fresh poison. How am I to reconcile this?"

"Please do not look so amazed, my lord. I despise the custom of vengeance, aye, but am willing to support you if you seek it. 'Tis your peace of mind with which I am concerned. I know you, good sir; your noble soul shall suffer great torment if you neglect to act upon this wrong. I will not stand by and see thee suffer!"

I step away from him and take up the last ingredient, a small jar of murky oil, which I hold poised above the bowl. "Now then, let us make haste to Claudius's chamber, to deliver this magnificent draft!"

"No."

"No?" My wrist snaps back; the drop that would bring death trembles a moment on the jar's lip, then slips within once more.

"Think on it, love," he whispers. "I have only the word of a ghost. A ghost that looks as my father looked, sounds as my father sounded, but still a ghost. Horatio did advise me that it might be some evil thing which only doth assume my father's form. I know not if I should trust it."

I move close to him and lay my hand upon his cheek. "What does the moon tell you?"

"That my ghost is honest. That Claudius did design this evil. But still I would have proof." He surprises me with a smile. "I do not believe the courts would accept the moon's account as reliable."

I bite back a grin of my own. "Most likely not." He is right, of course. Sighing, I return the jar of oil to my shelf. "Have you a plan, then?"

"A piece of one," says Hamlet, crossing to the bed and sitting. "Though I am hoping to enlist your assistance."

"It is yours. Tell me what you've contrived thus far."

"As earlier I told Horatio, I shall behave as though I am mad. I will show myself to be other than I am, appearing to suffer strange distemper. I shall put an antic disposition on. For it is possible the King will reveal his dark treachery in time—through some slip of speech, or by an unintended mention of the deed. My feigned incompetence just might facilitate such a slip."

"Oh, it is brilliance," I pronounce, clapping my hands. "You will elicit the King's confession with false madness! Claudius and all will believe your comprehension limited, your judgment askew; therefore, he will not suspect that you suspect and, therefore, will sooner divulge his secret."

"You understand!" Hamlet allows a grin. "Only when there remains no question of his guilt will I take action."

"It is genius, my lord."

"Madness and genius are close cousins, love." His smile falters. "And yet . . ."

Hamlet's heavy breath causes the flames to tremble on the candles.

"Yet what, my lord?"

"Well, I would ask thee not allow this be made known to any of the dull-witted, war-mongering men of this earth, but I, like you, have little love of vengeance."

"Now I am confused. Will you kill him or not?"

"Aye . . ." Hamlet closes his eyes. ". . . Nay." He drags one hand across his face in frustration. "I cannot say. I do not know."

"Do not bother yourself with it now, my lord. I trust you will do the honorable thing when the moment calls for it. To begin, it's as sound a scheme as it can be, having madness at its core. And I believe I have already begun to assist you in it."

Hamlet kisses my hair. "How do you help, love?"

"My lord, did you not this very night admit that if you do not soon have me you will indeed go mad?"

Hamlet throws back his head and laughs—a rugged noise that sends a shiver to my spine. And then, with only the breaking dawn to witness it, he brings his lips to mine.

There is a tender invitation in his kisses, and I discover that a choice is a changeable thing; I will be sure to tell as much to Anne.

I do not know how many hours pass that I am in his arms. But this much is certain—if Hamlet is mad, I am not to blame.

❦ ❦ ❦

Together, we have planned how 'twill begin, and now I tell of it to Anne.

We are deep in the kitchen, alone at midmorning, and she is spicing oldish mutton with saffron and pepper in an attempt to make it edible. For my part, I cannot keep my hands off the figs, or the almonds which await nearby in small piles. Anne has a smudge of cinnamon on her chin, and smells as lovely as she looks.

"Henceforth," I explain, biting into the sugary flesh of a fig, "Hamlet will put forth a plagued appearance. He will wander Elsinore as a man who is lost—in time and in place and in purpose. He shall ramble on in riots of words which will only skim the calm surface of sanity as stones across a quiet pool."

"So he will speak nonsense?"

"Aye."

"There is not much new in that."

I roll an onion across the wooden table. "There is more."

"Pray tell."

"Hamlet will handle me poorly."

Anne stops spicing. "He would harm you, Lia?"

"Nay! But I will seem to suffer his moods more directly, for we will lead everyone to believe that I am the cause of them."

"You will pretend Hamlet is crazed with love unrequited?"

"That is it. And in his madness, he will treat me, in varying degrees, with indifference, adoration, loathing, longing, and cruelty. It will be merely a pretense."

I rest my elbows on the rough-hewn tabletop, drop my chin in my hands, and watch Anne use her greasy thumb to swipe a lock of hair from her face. "This noon, in a most agitated state, I shall to my father's chamber make, where I will express to him that Hamlet has just made me a most improper visit. I, acting near crazed myself, will describe in Hamlet a most peculiar attitude, reporting that he was wild-eyed but silent, disheveled in dress, and distressed in demeanor. I will feign great fear of him."

Anne lets out a small snort of laughter. "That is a good one, verily!"

"'Tis true. This will be a most difficult role to play. God's truth, I do not know how I will bring my mouth to form but one unflattering word about him!"

"Imagine that you speak of Barnardo, then," advises Anne. "I daresay, that one is a few knights short of a crusade."

I smile. "He is an oaf, to be sure."

"Aye." Anne's eyes darken. "To be sure."

Now I am alert. "What is it?"

"'Tis nothing." She shakes her head.

I straighten up to take her shoulders and turn her to face me. "What hath Barnardo done to thee?"

"He's done naught, but not for lack of trying." Sighing, she wipes her hands on her skirt. "When I left your room yesternight, I met him on the stairs. To be polite, I bid him a good evening and smiled. Apparently, he took it to mean more than mere manners, for the next moment found me up against the wall."

"Roughly . . . ?"

"Aye. His hold was steady, and he was kissing my neck and shoulders as though he'd been invited to do so."

"God's mercy, Anne!" I throw my arms around her and squeeze, then pull back and look her in the eye. "Why did you not fight him?"

"Well, for one thing," says Anne, rolling her eyes, "the man carries a sword. All things considered, Lia, I thought it far better to have my throat kissed than slit!"

"So you allowed it?"

"What choice had I?"

"Uuhhcckk."

"Indeed, uhck! Although I believe Barnardo actually thought I was enjoying myself and was grateful for his advances. He is either too full of himself or too stupid to imagine otherwise."

"But, Anne!" I clasp her hands, ignoring the oily residue which clings to them. "You did nothing to incite this behavior!"

She shrugs. "I did smile."

"That does not give him such right as to molest you!"

"No, it does not. But he is a soldier, Lia, and I am a servant." Calmly, she shakes free of my hands and goes back to her task. "It happens. I just count myself lucky that it was not worse. It has been, you know, for others."

At that, my skin goes cold. I did not know. Could my father have been correct when he called me "green" and "unsifted"—naïve?

"Women of my station . . ." Anne begins, rubbing pepper into a slick, graying slice of mutton, "must tolerate this sort of thing. We exist, to men's minds, only to be of use to them . . . and in any number of ways, some bearable, some vile. But men believe that it is to them to decide. And we have little means of defying that."

My jaw drops. "You don't believe that!" I gasp. "You cannot have spent as many years in my company as you have and still believe that."

"It is not so much that I believe it, as that I accept it." Anne gives me a sad smile. "It is not the same for us, Lia. You are a lady. A well-born, beautiful lady. You are protected by your birth. I, though . . ." She sighs. "I am just one who doctors rotting meat."

"That is not so! You are more."

"To thee, perhaps. And for that, you have my love." Silence fills the kitchen. Finally, Anne draws a deep breath and says, "Go on."

"There is to be a note, written in the Prince's hand, to me."

"What manner of note?"

"A letter which describes Lord Hamlet's love! A love in all its mad grandeur. A love fit to punish, to poison."

"But to what purpose, this letter?" asks Anne. "It is no secret that you and Hamlet each have it badly for the other."

"Ah! But this note will be writ as a most puzzling piece of poetry. And since my father has denied me be near Hamlet, or speak to Hamlet, or—oh, the old fool— even think on Hamlet, he will leap to conclude that it is none but my avoidance that causes Hamlet to express himself so wildly, and without reason. Then, as he has such poor regard for me, he will surely present me to Claudius as a pawn in proving good Hamlet's ill-state."

"So this note shall be the proof that Hamlet's missing mind was lost in his pursuit of you?"

I nod.

Anne gives me a long look. "Would you know what I think, Lia?"

"Yes."

"I think you're *both* mad, and need no note to confirm my suspicions!"

I give her hand a playful slap.

"And that is the entire plan?"

"Aye. Unless events arise to alter it."

"And what of Horatio? Hath he a role in this deception?"

"Only to keep silent on't."

"And me?"

"Oh, we may have use for you," I tell her. "Later."

"Later?"

"When Hamlet kills the King."

Anne blinks at me once, twice, then her knees crumble and she is facedown in a platter of figs.

🩷 🩷 🩷

Anne is lying on a cot in her grim room adjacent to the larder. I have removed her stockings and elevated her feet. She is an amusing sight. I struggle not to laugh.

"Lia, I do not see what you find so comical! Murder is a sin unsurpassed."

"This is not murder, this is vengeance."

"You split hairs!" Anne draws the coverlet to her chin and frowns.

"I don't. Men do."

"I'll have none of it."

"Yes, you will," I tell her calmly, standing and handing her her slippers. "But let us not talk on it now." I move to the door.

"Where are you going?" she asks.

"To meet my dearest Hamlet at the stream." I smile at her over my shoulder. "We've a letter to compose."

## CHAPTER FOUR

WE ARE TOGETHER ON THE BANK OF THE STREAM. It glistens and tumbles and splashes itself, shallow in spots, deeper in others. In the distance, the sun throws long shadows from the towers of Elsinore.

On the opposite bank, I notice a figure, a man in dusty clothes, with a spade on his shoulder. He walks at a jaunty, almost musical pace. When he reaches the point directly across the stream from us, he turns and lifts his spade in a friendly salute.

I can see the dark lashes that rim his eyes from here. I wave.

"Who is that?" I ask.

Hamlet tilts his head backward. "Ah. The gravedigger. I've heard him sing."

"A singing gravedigger?"

"He is."

"That is an unlikely combination."

Hamlet nods.

I watch the man as he climbs the small hill that swells beyond the stream, away from Elsinore. There is a path down the other side which leads to the graveyard. Anne and I explored there once as girls; Laertes and Hamlet followed and frightened us near to death!

"I have never seen him," I say, more to myself than to Hamlet. "And yet he seems familiar."

Hamlet has not heard. I return to my teasing of him with a grass blade, leading it toward his temple, then sweeping small circles around his ear. He is ticklish there.

"Stop." It is not an order, but a plea.

"'Tis fun."

Laughing, he catches the weapon of my attack between his fingers and tears the blade in two. "We will accomplish nothing, lady, if you continue this torture." Hamlet rolls to his side and picks up a quill. "What shall we write in this letter? I cannot decide." His eyes darken in self-accusation, and he adds, "I can never decide."

"That is not true, my lord. You never have trouble deciding how best to make me smile."

He grins his gratitude, and reaches for me.

"The letter," I remind him.

"Yes. How will it begin?"

"Dear Ophelia."

"Too plain. Perhaps . . ." He thinks. "'To the celestial, and my soul's idol, the most beautiful Ophelia'?"

"Oh!" My heart beomes a thousand glittering butter-flies! I imagine they escape my body on the shine of my eyes. "That's a pretty phrase; 'beautiful' is a lovely word."

"I am glad that you are pleased."

"But we must change it."

"Change what is pretty and lovely?"

"Just by the breadth of a few letters, just enough to allow for misunderstanding. You may call me the most *beautified* Ophelia. Implying that there may be falsehood in my beauty."

"Clever girl." Hamlet writes it. "And then . . . ?"

"Well," I say, plucking another stalk of grass and wrap-ping it round my finger. "If you are to convince Claudius that you are mad for love, you must compose lines to indi-cate that you love madly."

"I do love madly," says Hamlet.

I blush, liking his honesty and the ease with which he attests to this. "That is good to hear, my lord. But we're wanting to show that love has tricked you outside of your-self. That love has knocked you senseless."

"That is the truth." He smiles. Then a ragged breath escapes him. "I only wish there were more truths alive at Elsinore. I so greatly hate the lies."

"The lies, my lord?" A chill wind whips through, and I move closer to his warmth. "I do not believe it is the lies of which we should be wary."

"What mean you?"

"I mean that the lies merely disguise what is the plentiful truth, and the truth of this situation is a far greater danger than the lie."

He looks at me a moment. "You are keen, my love. I had not thought on it as such."

"We ourselves are about to lie, are we not?"

His eyes get warm. "Again, love?"

"You are shameless!" I tell him, laughing. "You know my meaning is that we are about to compose a lie in this letter!"

"Yes. So let us have at it. 'Most beautified Ophelia. You must not doubt my love.' How sounds that?"

"Sane, sir, unfortunately. But you give me an idea. Wouldn't mad love cause one to doubt what is surely undoubtable? Could love so true be so beyond doubtless as to render even the undoubtable doubtful by comparison?"

Hamlet shifts a look at me. "If that does not convey a damaged mind, I do not know what will."

"Precisely! Write this: 'Doubt thou the stars . . . doth shimmer on high.'"

Hamlet puts pen to parchment, then halts. "Or 'Doubt thou the stars are fire.' How is that?"

"Oh, that is even better! Go on."

"Doubt . . . that the sun doth move."

"Yes! Beauteous, my lord. 'Twould be nice if it could rhyme!"

Hamlet frowns. "Is that not a little much, love?"

I lift my chin, pretend a pout. "I've always wished for a love letter in rhyming verse."

"Then you shall have one." He grumbles in concentration a moment; then his pen moves again. "'Doubt . . . truth . . . to be . . . a liar. But never doubt . . . I love.'"

"More . . ."

"'O dear Ophelia, I am ill at these numbers. . . .'"

"No, sir, you are quite the opposite—you prove yourself quite talented at writing verse!"

He taps the parchment with the quill point. "I want to say, somehow, that in your arms our sighs do come in such great amounts that I am hopeless even to count them."

"Yes, that is lovely, Hamlet. Try this: 'I have not art to reckon . . .'"

The quill flies across the page. "'. . . art to reckon . . .'"

"'My groans.'"

"'My . . .'" His head snaps up, and his eyes lock on mine. Beneath them is a smile. "Groans, lady?"

"Groans, sire. Remember, you are meant to be mad. A madman would bar no honesty from his verse."

"Honesty is one thing, sweet. This is sheer wantonness." He laughs, shrugs, writes: "'I have not art to reckon my groans . . . but . . . but that I love thee best, O most best, believe it.'" Hamlet lifts his gaze to me and repeats, "I love thee best. Believe it."

"Pray, let that not be a piece of the made-up madness."

"I have never been more lucid," he promises, "more sure, or more sound." He sweeps me into his arms and holds me. "What would your father say, were he to know that you do see me after he's forbidden it?"

"He would be angry," I say calmly.

"And angrier still if he knew . . . if he knew you plan to wed one who will kill a king."

I lean away and study Hamlet closely. "You are worried."

"Aye. It began the moment my father's ghost did will this task to me. 'Tis the burden of my birth—to set this villainy to right. And though I may loathe the custom of revenge, I loathe foul Claudius more. And yet . . ."

"Yet?"

"It is a decision that all but grinds the enamel from my teeth."

"But there is no decision, sir, for the decision has been made for you."

"By a ghost?"

"Nay, by history!" I clasp his hand. "By centuries of backward-thinking sons of murdered fathers. Their grim legacy is visited upon your soul, and for that I pity you. It is not right, but it is done, and needs be done again."

"Aye." He nods, a heavy nod. "I will kill the King. But 'tis most difficult to act swiftly when regret does slow my blood."

"Talk not to me of difficulty, good sir, until you have lived but one day as a woman."

At last, a smile, or part of one at least. "Which brings me to the question of my mother's response to all of this. She herself has become a question without answer, now a monster in mine eyes, and yet, as well, an angel. Victim of Claudius, to be certain, but also of her own feminine frailty."

My mouth turns down at him. "I prefer we talk not on your notion of frailty and women, sir. In fact, I warn thee—go not there."

"I have never called you frail, love," he assures me. "Indeed, I can think of no more preposterous falsehood."

"You are wise to say so, Hamlet. And now tell me of Fortinbras."

He looks surprised. "You know of Fortinbras?"

I nod.

"I thought you had no appreciation for war."

"Appreciation, my lord, is other than interest, and what does with thee is ever of utmost concern to me. I know that Fortinbras does march from Norway to avenge his father's death and to conquer Elsinore, which means he would surely take your life—and, in so doing, mine as well."

"That, love, I could not bear. Do not trouble thyself with thoughts of Norway. I am assured by my father's advisers that 'twill not amount to much."

He kisses my forehead, then looks to the clouded sun, and finds the hour growing late. He stands, brushes the dry grass from his tunic and hose, then helps me to my feet.

"You know what you are to do now?"

"I do, sir," I answer. "But I would linger here a moment to gather my thoughts and prepare for this role. You will find me in the castle anon. And ready."

Hamlet nods, stuffing the parchment into my palm. He places a kiss upon my mouth, then whispers in my ear:

*"Days hence, together we shall confess these necessary sins.*
*Let madness now protect this vengeful Prince. So it begins."*

ఈ ఈ ఈ

When he is gone, I remain beside the stream for a time, enjoying the crispness of the breeze and the memories that accompany it. The stream glistens; farther down it swells to become a crystalline pool, surprisingly wide, dangerously deep, in which my mother taught me to swim when I was but four in years. We always swam in secret, as the old beliefs often cited the ability to float a characteristic of witches. My lady mother found this laughable; it had always seemed to her that the black, leaden soul of a sorceress would surely cause her to sink like a stone rather than float. Buoyancy, she said, was surely more akin to goodness.

Only Laertes and Anne know that I swim. Not even Hamlet is aware of it.

There is a cluster of winter flowers growing round a stone near the stream, a type I do not recognize. I collect them, and will consult my volume later for their name.

At last, I turn to begin the journey back to Elsinore; I take a step . . . then another. . . . Then stop, compelled to turn again to face the brook, and beyond.

He is there, atop the hill, and I see him as clearly as though he were but a foot in front of me.

The gravedigger.

And he is singing.

ℰ ℰ ℰ

"Oh, my lord, my lord . . ."

My father whirls when I fling myself into his room. I have loosened my hair from its pins, pinched my cheeks to draw a troubled hue, and I breathe deeply in a broken rhythm.

"I have been so affrighted!"

"With what, in the name of God?"

Pressing my palm to my bosom, I tell him that Hamlet came to my room whilst I was sewing. I describe the Prince in a state of near undress, with his shirt open, his stockings falling slack. He was pale, I tell my father, and his knees did knock together as though from fear.

Polonius leans toward me with his mouth agape, his hands reaching as if for the next word I will add to this ghastly description.

"Mad for thy love?"

I am momentarily stunned. That was almost too easy! He is already imagining according to our design.

"My lord," I say, with heaving breaths, "I do not know." Then I add, "But truly I do fear it."

"What said he?"

I close my eyes, as though to remember—this scene that ne'er happened.

"He took me by the wrist," I impart, "and held me hard."

Dramatically, I lay my arm against my forehead. Polonius gasps at my re-enactment. He is an easy mark!

"Long stayed he so," I tell him. "At last . . . he raised a sigh so piteous and profound that it did seem to shatter all his bulk and end his being."

I describe his departure from my room—Hamlet holding his gaze on me as he made his exit, as though he could not bear to pull his eyes from mine.

Polonius is in a state. He paces the room, his arms flailing.

"Come, go with me! I will go seek the King."

He catches my arm and tugs, while I pretend a puzzled look.

"This is the very ecstasy of love!" he cries, then stops and faces me with knitted brow. "What, have you given him any hard words of late?"

"No, my good lord!" (Such an innocent look I would not have believed I could muster.) "But, as you did command, I did repel his letters and denied his access to me."

I hand him the note, which he devours with his eyes, and I can see, even as he reads, that his thoughts pivot on his own significance; he pays no heed to mine.

My father bids me wait in an empty hall whilst he searches out the King.

"Pssst."

"Anne?"

She approaches on tiptoe. "I have been listening to Claudius and Gertrude. They converse with fellows of the Prince, friends from his blithe childhood. Mayhap you remember them—Rosey Plants and Gilded Lily."

"Do you mean Rosencrantz and Guildenstern?"

"Yes. It is them. The taller one has lovely curls."

"And the shorter?"

"Nice teeth."

"Have they come to mourn the father of their friend? Do they seek to comfort Hamlet in his grief?"

Anne shakes her head. "They come at the behest of Claudius."

"Touching what purpose?"

"To spy on gentle Hamlet."

"Devil take it! The King . . ."

"And Queen."

"She is in on it as well? Arrggh! She is beyond frailty, then. She is false! She plots against her own son. Have Rosencrantz and Guildenstern agreed?"

"Aye, they have."

"The curs! The dogs! Oh, there is a plague of disloyalty

upon this castle!" I stamp my foot. "Damn Rosencrantz and Guildenstern to hell! The only benevolence is that their wretched treachery will serve to expedite our efforts in proving the Prince is mad."

Anne frowns. "So you are glad for their presence?"

"Glad that they will corroborate our deception. Furious that they betray Hamlet's most excellent esteem so easily."

"Besides lovely curls and nice teeth," Anne says, "men have little to recommend them."

How to proceed? My brow does crease in thought. "Dear Anne, will you find my love? Will you tell him what you've heard regarding his fellows, so that he may behave appropriately when he does meet them?"

"As you wish, Lia. I shall tell him all I heard."

"Godspeed, then."

She departs, her slippers scuffing the stones. Then—an approaching commotion. I shield myself round a corner, to bend mine eye upon my father. He makes a windy entrance as he leads the King and Queen, talking—nay, rambling—about Hamlet as he comes!

"Your noble son," he states, "is mad."

He withdraws the note, Hamlet's and mine, and reads the words aloud.

Gertrude hears, transfixed. "Came this from Hamlet to her?" she asks.

Polonius confirms it, and then I am interrupted from behind by a kiss to my shoulder. I turn to face my love. His hair is tousled—oh, beauteous—and he carries a book.

"Hush," I tell him, pointing round to where his mother-aunt and uncle-father endure Polonius's palaver.

"Kissing is quiet," he tells me, placing another on my neck.

"Hath Anne met with you?" I ask.

"On the issue of my guests who come as spies? Aye, she has."

"You are prepared, then."

"As ever I shall be. 'Tis another cut into my heart. Thank God that you exist to mend it."

And then Anne comes skidding in, breathless. Her eyes fix Hamlet with a cautious look. "Are you certain, lady, that this man is not genuinely mad?"

I glance a narrowed gaze at Hamlet, who lifts one shoulder in a gesture so casual I know he's committed some friendly mischief on Anne.

"What hath he done, Anne?"

"Turned cartwheels, for one! Kicking his feet skyward and rolling over himself on his hands. And singing all the while! Wild-eyed and laughing one moment, then sobbing the next."

"I thought," he confesses, shrugging, "that she might be a good one on whom to rehearse my madness."

Poor, gullible Anne! Even as she knew the game was afoot, she believed my love was ill. I turn to Hamlet. "You are good."

"I am better." He winks at me, then reaches for Anne's hand, to which he presses a most courtly kiss. "My dear one, I've yet to thank you for the delicious mutton enjoyed at this noon's dinner. And more thanks come to you for apprising me of the King's deceitful usage of my friends." He withdraws his book, which he has tucked beneath his arm, and slaps it softly. "I go now to perform."

"Do it well, my lord," I wish him.

## CHAPTER FIVE

ALONE IN MY CHAMBER, I EXAMINE THE NEW
plants I gathered near the river.

There is a spiky quality to the leaves, which are a green that
falls somewhere between bright and mellow. I brush them
against my palm, and wonder what properties they hold.

I break off one lacy leaf and tear it into pieces, which I
sprinkle in a crucible. Then I find my flint, bring forth a small
flame, and use a dry twig to ignite the contents of the bowl.

The smoke rises in whitish whirls, like windblown wisps
of fairy hair.

Sweet, so sweet, this scent. Earth's aroma, pungent-fresh
and woodsy-green, and warm.

The smoke billows, lifting to caress my face and settle in
my hair; it stings my eyes, but only slightly, as tears of gladness might.

I breathe in deeply as the world wavers.

Oh, wondrous,

Oh, wishful,

Why and wherefore . . .

How numb! How filled with feeling, and yet how numb! My fingertips tingle as they gather diamonds from this haze. And then the mist makes shadows of itself, and then again within itself, and there, in the smoke, is a daydream that is not at all a daydream but a figure, aye, a shape— with eyes and lips and fragile chin. And hair, unbound and strung with flowers, flowing as mine flows when the cool stream in summer shimmers round me while I swim . . .

Swim . . .

Through the smoke,

Through the sparkling stream,

To my mother.

My mother. Who speaks.

She speaks! With a lonely lilt and yet ethereal joy in her voice. *"Ophelia."*

'Tis my mother's saintly spirit! Oh, blessed mercy, can this be so? She extends her pretty arms and smiles.

I would run to her, but the smoke distorts the room as though I must cross a plain too broad, too narrow, too solid, and too soft.

*"Ophelia . . ."*

The word enters me at my heart, and I am at once so filled with love and longing that I expect my soul to burst forth from my breast.

"Lady?" I whisper, then again I part my lips and the word sings itself: "Mother?"

The apparition nods.

"Why do you come?"

The spirit, my mother, steps forward—it is as a sunbeam shimmering on water.

*"Child. Daughter. Woman. You are all of these, and lovely at each."*

"With all credit gone to you, dear lady. For 'twas you taught me to be who I am, and all who knew you say that I am nothing if not your very image."

I feel pride radiate from her lightness, and then sadness intervenes. *"I come because Polonius does cause you great pain."*

In the haze, the hurt comes back—his disregard, his pure indifference.

"Yes," I answer on a sob.

*"Hear me, dear one. Listen well. Though I fear what follows may cut as certainly as it cures, I must impart to you a truth—I pray you will find comfort in't, even as I know it will stun thee."*

The smoke curls, and for a moment she is gone. But she returns, and her voice carries as clearly as peals of church bells through thin morning air.

*"He is not yours."*

The figure falters in the mist, and again she is near lost. Light calls upon darkness, and together they churn before my eyes. I reach for my mother; again she speaks.

*"You are not his."*

"I am not . . . whose?" I shut my eyes to summon thought. The smoke invades me at every pore, and with it an understanding, a most marvelous reckoning. "Polonius!" I cry. "He is not mine. I am not his!"

The ghost replies in silence so profound I know there is only truth between us. O in the name of all that is holy, I can scarce contain my relief!

Polonius.

Is.

Not.

My.

Father.

Breath comes up short, and I spin inside myself.

"Sweet, gracious ghost, tell me, please, shall I believe this?"

Her speech is moonbeams and lark song and stars. *"If it heals thee, Ophelia, then, aye, believe it. If it brings thee greater pain, then believe it not—you need not take our secret beyond this mist. You may leave it here to vanish with this sleepy smoke."*

My eyes flutter. "This smoky sleep . . ."

*"I would beg your forgiveness,"* the spirit says.

"Forgive thee?" I cry in joyous disbelief. "For telling now this secret? Nay, this sudden truth does lift in me bubbles of irreconcilable happiness. For he . . . is . . . not . . . mine!"

Laughter tumbles forth from me, and I am helpless to resist it. I am grateful and weak with the freedom brought by this news; my senses abandon me until laughter is all there is. Laughter.

"Oh, if I be unloved, unloved I am by one who hath no reason to love me at all." I offer my gaze to the apparition.

"Tell me, lady, Mother, ghost, and friend, what of Laertes? Does he share this fate, and if he does, do we also share our father?"

*"Aye."*

"And do I know him?"

*"You will."*

"Pray, how?"

*"By his singing."*

And now I hear the voice—a rich and distant manly timbre. The singing wraps around me with the smoke.

"Am I the child of one who would love me if he knew?"

*"That is most certain."*

And now the vision ripples in the smoke.

My chamber door opens and Anne appears; I see her through the shimmering image of the ghost before me.

*"Ophelia . . ."*

"Ophelia!"

My mother's voice is one with Anne's. Yes, Anne is here. She is beating at the mist with her hands, coughing, throwing back the fur covering at the window.

"Lia? Wake! Please."

I open my eyes to Anne. They sting, and she looks as though she is melting. "Anne?"

She leans over me.

"Good lady, do you breathe?"

I sit up slowly. "Most excellent well," I tell her through heavy lips. "My head throbs slightly, but . . ."

"Lia, there is a most rank odor in here." She finds the smoldering crucible and dumps its scorched contents from the window.

"Actually"—I am enjoying the tingling of my fingertips—"I believe I found it . . . pleasant."

"Pleasant? I daresay, Lia, this smoke hath removed you from your mind."

"No, friend," I tell her, looking to the spot where my mother stood. "I daresay it has restored me to my heart."

❦ ❦ ❦

My chamber has been cleared of smoke, and Anne hath rinsed the stale aroma from my hair using water scented with a blend of lemongrass and lavender. I sit beside the fire and coax away the snarls with my fingers.

"There is news of a play," Anne tells me. "A troupe arrived not two hours ago, and are meant to perform tomorrow night."

"Players!" I grumble. "This castle verily crawls with players, and the King be the worst of them."

We are interrupted by a knock, which Anne answers. I am aware of an exchange of whispers.

"The Prince sends word," she reports, reaching for my gown. "You will meet him in the outer bailey—now."

I spring from my stool to step into the gown's billowing skirt, and shove my arms into the snug sleeves. Then I pull on my cloak, and away.

We meet in moonlight's faint beginnings 'neath an early-evening sky. It is bitter in the bailey shadows where we hide. Hamlet tells me of his meeting with Polonius, how he played at madness so completely that the man did quake within his shoes.

"Tell me of this discourse," I demand. "Leave naught to my imagining. I would know every furrow of confusion in his ignoble brow."

Hamlet rests his chin upon my hair. "I called him a fishmonger, to start."

"Wise of you."

"One must always be wise when one is mad."

"Go on."

"I carried with me a book, and Polonius did ask what I read. I told him, 'Words, words, words.'"

"'Twas a silly answer."

"Aye, but 'twas a silly question. What else could one read but words?"

"Think you he's convinced, then?" I ask.

"I do."

"And what of Rosencrantz and Guildenstern? Think they too that you are . . . shall we say, several fathoms shallow of a full moat?"

Hamlet laughs. "Aye. Methinks they do, though they are uncertain of what causes my mental drought."

"Perhaps it shall rain sanity soon," I tease.

"But already I am in it too deeply, love. Indeed, I over-run with reason."

"Now, what of the play?"

"The play," says Hamlet. "'Twill entertain us tomorrow evening. I confess, I've altered the production. Know you *The Murder of Gonzaga*? They will perform it, however, with a change. They will enact the very tale told to me by my father's ghost."

"Ah!" I nod. "You are beyond reasonable, sir, you are brilliant. Art which imitates life shall be the King's accuser, and upon seeing his crime enacted, foul Claudius will surely recognize that he is known!"

"It will unsettle him surely, mayhap extract from him a full admission."

"You are shrewd, sweet Hamlet," I whisper, running my palm o'er the roughness of his cheek. "Yes. The play will be the very thing, wherein you shall expose and catch the conscience of the King!"

"That, my darling one," he whispers, drawing my face toward his, "is precisely how I said it."

ॐ ॐ ॐ

Next morning, I am awakened harshly by Polonius.

"Up, woman. Your lord has use for you."

I stumble, for sleep still floats itself across the surface of my understanding. My mouth is dry, my eyes do battle with the light of day. Cool air ripples along the flesh beneath my flannel gown, and I shiver. "What do you wish of me?"

"You will follow me now to the great hall," he orders.

"May I ask the purpose, sir?"

"Prince Hamlet hath been summoned there. You will arrive as well, a seemingly accidental encounter. King Claudius and I will conceal ourselves and observe this planned-chance meeting. From such observance shall we ascertain the extent of Hamlet's affliction. If love for you hath made him mad, the proof will produce itself there in your troubling presence."

"Just yesterday you forbade me speak to Hamlet. Now you command me meet him in the hall at dawn!"

"Think not to challenge me. Do as I insist. Now dress!" He turns and makes to leave, then turns again to face me. "Mark me, girl. Do not dream to inform the Prince of this intrigue! You will not send your maid to tell him prior, nor shall you yourself during the course of the confrontation, give any signal with your eyes or lips or hands to warn him that we watch." He glares at me. "Know, Ophelia, this guilt is yours. 'Tis the fault of your most reckless beauty that Denmark suffers. Your welcome willingness inspired him, and now he finds you unwilling to be welcoming. This confuses his heart and poisons his mind."

Anger bristles within me. "'Twas you who turned my will unwilling, sir! Must I remind you of that?"

My insolence causes him to bare his teeth. "I discouraged your encouragement, for in my wisdom I knew that what you might do would be his undoing."

"Had I remained willing," I mutter, "and done what I would do, his undoing would not be done."

Polonius looks blank, then sputters, for my words rattle his empty mind. "Curse the day the Prince laid eyes upon you."

He storms from the room. I pluck a simple gray gown from the back of a chair and slip it over my head, pausing to touch the chain and charm so recently given me by my love. I am not afraid, I am thrilled to the depths of my soul! Another chance to deceive those who have so deceived the Prince.

☙ ☙ ☙

We join the others: Claudius and Gertrude, their accomplices, Rosencrantz and Guildenstern—curly hair and nice teeth but no honor between them. The King and Queen interrogate their spies, who reveal little. Hamlet may be mad; then, mayhap, not; but if so, they've concluded nothing of the cause. Claudius bids them continue the search; they agree and are off.

"Sweet Gertrude, leave us too," says Claudius, and explains the forced encounter that is to come.

I watch the Queen's eyes whilst she listens, surprised when she turns to me a gentle countenance.

"Ophelia, I hope your virtues will bring Hamlet to his wonted way again, to both your honors."

I nod, swallowing words I long to say. Would that I could break the spell her husband casts and show to her the wickedness that surrounds this scene. But I cannot, for I've only one role to play this morn. "Madam," I whisper, "I wish it may."

She takes her leave, and my almost-father gives me my direction.

"Ophelia, walk you here." He hands to me, of all things, a book of prayers, suggesting that my reading such will give purpose to my being about alone.

Claudius and my father withdraw to witness. In moments, Hamlet draws nigh. I look up from my missal, and the breath is all but gone from my body. He carries his beauty most dangerously this morn—tousled hair and hooded eyes. He approaches as though he sees me not, and speaks aloud to none, to all.

*"To be, or not to be—that is the question. . . ."*

His passion draws me in. My eyes are wide, my lips parted and trembling. It is poetry, pure and dark, and deathish. I have never heard such words as these from Hamlet. He speaks a truth, disguised by madness, and together they chill my blood. Has he thought upon this sin before? Has the notion of giving himself over to an always sleep occurred to him before this game? And dare I confess it hath occurred to me? On the day I lost my mother, aye.

The gravedigger. Did he sing that day when I returned alone to the freshly scarred earth beneath which my mother lay? I heard him, aye! Did not I wish to follow her on that most mystical journey to anywhere but here? And did my father's cold and callused hand clamp firmly on my shoulder without ever reaching to wipe a tear?

Hamlet turns to face me, cutting short his speech.

I nod at him. "Good my lord, how does Your Honor for this many a day?" On impulse, I remove the gilt pendant from my throat and hold it out to him. I feel my father's wicked wonderment, the King's concern.

"My lord," I say, effecting a tremble so that the chain sounds a hollow jangle between my fingers. "I have remembrances of yours that I have longed long to redeliver." As I extend my hand, the pendant slices a shaft of sunlight, exploding in brightness. "I pray you, now receive them."

Hamlet gazes at the charm and tosses off a shrug of pure indifference. "No, not I," he murmurs. "I never gave you aught."

I widen my eyes, and shake my head. "My honored lord, you know right well you did. . . ." I press the precious pendant in his palm, and finish firmly. "There, my lord."

I pray the spies see not the sparks that surely fly at Hamlet's touch, his chain, our chain, clutched between my hand and his. He does not let go as he frowns hard at me and asks me if I'm honest.

I pretend to be stunned. I know he means two words with one—with "honest" he inquires if I be truthful, and also, more scathingly, if I be chaste. He alone knows the answer to both. I plump my lower lip as though I may begin to weep and respond in a quivering voice:

"My lord?"

"Are you fair?"

"What means Your Lordship?"

And now, with fiery speech, he begins a wordy tempest in which he scolds me for my beauty, and insists there can be no honesty in one so beautiful.

"I did love you once!" he roars.

I stammer in reply, "Indeed, my lord, you made me believe so."

Now he begins to pace, a purposeless march around me, so that I must spin on the spot where I stand to keep my eyes on him. One hand is clenched in a fist around the necklace, the other he drags through his hair as he hollers, "You should not have believed me. . . . I loved you not!"

A wail comes unbidden from my throat. Even in this fantasy I cannot bear to hear it. Tears surprise me, and I bellow in return, "I was the more deceived."

"Get thee to a nunnery" is his evil command. "Why wouldst thou be a breeder of sinners?"

Were I not so schooled upon this task, I would laugh. Ordering me to a convent! I can hear Polonius gasping in the shadows. Hamlet does well enacting madness. And his talk of breeding brings a blush to my cheek, for we at length have talked and dreamed of the children we shall have—sturdy sons for him to spoil, and daughters, all darling, to dote on—as many as the good Lord sees fit to grant us. We have imagined their laughter ringing through the halls of Elsinore, the innocent touch of their sweet lips as they kiss us both good night.

Hamlet strokes his chin, then, counting on his fingers, he lists his faults: "I am very proud, revengeful, ambitious, with more offenses at my beck than I have thoughts to put them in, imagination to give them shape, or time to act them in."

And here he winks so only I can see! The joke, of course, is that he faults his own imagination. No one has more imagination than this Prince, and herein lies the proof! How gracefully these falsehoods fall from his lips! I conjure a look of utter dismay, covering my mouth with my hand (to keep from grinning), and allow my knees to buckle at the thought of his corruption.

With the spittle spraying from his mouth, he barks, "Where's your father?"

*Hiding 'neath the stairs,* I am thinking, but make my voice minuscule, as though his cruelty has stripped me of all esteem. "At home, my lord."

He shouts some more, ordering the doors shut upon Polonius, and I send up a fraudulent prayer. "Oh, help him, you sweet heavens!"

At last, with fists pounding the atmosphere, he makes a stormy exit, leaving me to close this performance. Seizing the opportunity, I fall to my knees, clutch my heart, and cry out, "Oh, what a noble mind is here o'erthrown!" I close my eyes and beat my fists against the stony floor.

When I look up again, I see Hamlet peering from around a corner. He rolls his eyes at me but smiles. I would stick my tongue out at him and remind him of his own theatrics, but he makes a soundless exit when the King approaches.

Polonius drags me upward from the stones.

And then—a sentence handed down upon me far worse than even death: the King declares that Hamlet go to England! My knees buckle now in earnest. When Claudius turns to Polonius to beg his opinion, I summon strength to flee.

Up a winding stair, and fleet across the stony floor to Hamlet's chamber, to tell him of Claudius's decree to banish him. We must now speed our plan to action and implicate the King. Surely that will save us.

I am poised to pound upon the door when it swings open.

"Hamlet . . ."

"Love!" He gathers me in his arms and twirls me. "Were we not most expert at our game? Aye, perhaps you did milk it overmuch at the finale. . . ."

(He chooses a poor time to be a critic!) "Good my lord, please . . ."

"And returning my gift, a stroke of pure cunning, that!" He reaches within his shirt to remove the jeweled pendant and replaces it around my neck. "Take care that no one sees it again gracing your gracious form, as it will upset the fragile balance of this plan."

"Understood, my lord, but, please . . ."

"Say naught," he says, then whispers, "We shall talk later, once the play is done. I must go now to meet the players to ensure they do their parts as I imparted."

With a kiss, he rushes off, leaving me alone to keep my grim news to myself.

I take it with me to the stream.

## CHAPTER SIX

IT IS AS THOUGH HE KNEW TO EXPECT ME, FOR HE
waits at the bank, singing.

The gravedigger. My father.

A great yearning yawns within me at the sight of him.
As I approach, I notice that his coat is plain, frayed at the
wrists, deeply stained with earth and grass. His hands too
seem ingrained with the good brown of fresh dirt. He
wears his work upon him, and I admire this. There is nothing ghoulish or macabre in his manner; rather, he has about
him a quiet sincerity, a kindness apropos of one who
assists others in mourning.

Closer now, I see how very much alike we are. My eyes
are surely a gift from him, and the long thin line of my
throat indeed resembles his. His hair is the same rich chest-
nut as Laertes' hair, and I recognize they have in common

a very uncommon squareness of the jaw. Oh, handsome is he!

He sings a ballad I've not heard before, as I gather stalks of withered green and slick yellow stems from which I pinch off dead blossoms. Beneath my feet the hedgemaids are crisp, and the rustle they make is a sound like applause.

At last, I speak. "God save you, sir, and a pleasant day to thee."

The gravedigger, my father, inclines his head. "And to thee, lady."

"You . . . knew my mother, I believe."

"Aye." He nods again. "Knew her. Loved her."

His frankness startles me, but only a moment. I bolster my own courage to ask, "Do you know me?"

"You are Ophelia."

The sound of my name on his lips is a comfort I can not describe! This, I understand, is a most particular piece of eternity we share. His eyes moisten with tears; mine, I am sure, already flow freely, though I am too numb to feel them.

"Shall we walk?" he asks, reaching for my arm.

"Aye."

The gravedigger, my father, leads me up a winding way to the crest of a small rise I remember all too well, though I have not been back to it near on two years now. It is my mother's grave, and I am not surprised to see how gently it has been tended.

"Blue vervain," I remark, brushing my fingers o'er the tips of the tall, slender flowers growing there; the candle-like wands bloom from bottom up, tiny bluish blossoms climbing heavenward like flame.

"'Tis said this flower grew on Mount Calvary," he says, "and 'twas used to dress the wounds of our Saviour."

"Yes," I tell him, nodding. "I've heard that. And these"—I crouch low to examine the brilliant red of a *Lobelia cardinalis*—"they are cardinal flowers, are they not?"

He nods, proudly. "Rare, this time of year especially."

"Indeed they are." I palm one graceful petal. "I've seen some doing poorly along the water's edge e'en in mid-summer. How is it they flourish here and now?"

"I coax the shoots from pots of soil I keep at home, then bring them to this sacred place and commend them to the earth."

I sigh. "They will not last, then."

"Things most rare and beautiful," he replies, touching the cross that marks my mother's grave, "are all too often all too brief."

"Oh!" My hand moves to a cluster of weeds. "*Eupatorium purpureum*," I cry, delighted.

"From the Latin," he says, standing taller, "meaning 'of a noble father.'"

"Yes, I grow it in my chamber! The weeds are homely but smell sugary when their leaves are crumbled."

"Your mother, saints rest her, loved the scent, and so I

grow them here." He bends beside me, plucking a pinkish flower. "They yield quite a cogent physic, you know. A medicinal antidote to most any manner of lethal poison."

I blink in surprise. "I did not know."

"Good to keep such knowledge handy," says he, adjusting his ragged cap.

"Verily." There is a pause. "Good sire, how came you to know my mother? Was she married when you met? Or was it when you were both younger? And why, pray tell, if she loved thee, would she bind herself to such an addle-pated knave as Polonius?"

He chuckles, deep in his throat. "You are a most inquisitive female, you are!"

"But I would know. I must know!"

"So you shall." The gravedigger's eyes go distant, and his voice is mild, musical. "We met just days after her father promised her to Polonius. I was, at that time, a traveling player, a minstrel, come to Elsinore with my troupe to entertain the good King Hamlet's court." He draws a quivering breath. "She was mayhap the age you are today. I loved her of an instant, and she swore the same feeling for me. But she could not disgrace her family by forsaking her betrothed. She despised him but could not bring dishonor to her family by running off with a mere player."

"And so?"

"And so . . . when my fellows departed, I stayed behind, took up a pickax, and commenced digging graves, only to be near her."

"And you were?"

"Of that," he says, with a playful pinch to my cheek, "you and your brother are the proof."

I smile. "I would know where you reside."

He jerks his thumb toward the far slope of the rise. "I've a small stone house at the end of the croft there. You will find it by the smoke that comes from its chimney."

"And the song that comes through its windows?"

He smiles. "Aye, daughter."

At this, I fling myself into his arms, and he holds me as though he's dreamed of doing it. "Daughter," he whispers against my hair.

From out of a dream, I feel another's arms surround me and know my mother's angelic spirit has witnessed this healing.

Together, we spend the afternoon. I tell him of Hamlet, and the strife alive at Elsinore.

He listens and offers his assistance, if e'er I require it.

Later, I depart with a plump bouquet of sweet purpureum; my father's ballad follows me with the sound of the stream.

And I prepare to see the play.

❦ ❦ ❦

I am excited and frightened to the depths of my soul.

The play is about to begin.

We sit together, I and Hamlet, and for the case of his

madness, he speaks to me so lewdly that it brings to his cheeks a faint blush that only I behold. At times I need urge him continue his sordid seduction. All who hear are o'erwhelmed and mortified that one formerly so gallant would speak such vulgar propositions.

The King watches Hamlet, and Hamlet watches the King.

And we all watch the play, unfolding in an argument familiar to the one murderer among us. I turn ever so slightly in my seat, just the breadth of breath, to bend mine eye on him.

Now the player upon the stage creeps silently toward his victim. Claudius, in robes of richest silk, goes pasty gray. I feel Hamlet tense beside me, and my heart aches, for I imagine he imagines this deed delivered upon his sire.

The player sweeps his arm in a silent circle round the head of his fellow who reclines upon a bench as though asleep amidst the garden. Claudius trembles, his eyes widen, water, bulge, and blink. Aye, 'tis a mirror in which he gapes. 'Tis art which imitates life, and also death.

The player-King produces, as though by magic, a jeweled cruet, which he holds aloft, then lowers, slow, so sinister and so slow, toward his fellow thespian's ear. He tips it so that the candlelight catches the trembling drop which falls from the spout like a tear. I shiver, lean near to Hamlet's warmth, but there is little. He's gone cold with the thought of what's to come. Wretched Claudius sees clearly his deed of evil in the enactment. At the moment the glittering trickle enters the actor's ear, Claudius leaps to his feet, wailing.

The audience gapes, and Gertrude holds her heart. "How fares my lord?"

A silly question! Ashen is he, and trembling, clutching his middle as though demons threaten to birth themselves from within him. He makes for the door. Hamlet squeezes my hand, then springs from his own seat in pursuit.

Shrieking, Claudius goes, calling for light. Hamlet is close upon his heels, gathering this victory. Around us, players turn up their palms in confusion, and the audience runs hither and yon with worry for their counterfeit lord.

I would go after Hamlet, to see how the condemnation finishes off the stricken King, but at Horatio's insistence I am swept away from the commotion roughly by the guard Barnardo.

"Remove her," shouts Horatio. "She will be harmed."

"I *am* harmed!" I respond, for Barnardo's callused hand grips my arm as though I am his prisoner.

"Take her to her closet," Horatio instructs.

There is a cruel glint in Barnardo's eyes as he drags me hard across the stones from the great hall toward the stairs. His dirty nails dig into my flesh, and a sickening heat doth radiate from his body near mine.

"Unhand me, sirrah," I snarl.

But he ignores it, yanking me off my feet to carry me to my room. Inside, he drops me in a heap upon my pallet.

"Barnardo! You forget yourself."

"I forget nothing," says he, his eyes at once vacant and menacing as they slide o'er me. "I forget not how you have cast your randy gaze at me. . . ."

"God's blood!" My eyes go round with scandalized disgust. "You will be punished for speaking to me so. I am a lady of this court!"

"Aye, and more enticing for it." His lips glisten as his tongue strokes them, then from those lips comes a most guttural sound I can only guess is meant to be a laugh. "I know you do desire me, Ophelia. For I have seen thee sigh and blush whene'er I pass."

Horror rises in me like bile. "Near blasphemy is that, Barnardo! If I've sighed in your presence, 'tis only out of pity that one could be so dull as thee."

He takes a rough hold of my chin and glares at me unkindly. "I will show you how dull I am," he growls.

A chill creeps upon my flesh, for his bawdy undertone is clear. I make to slap his face, but he catches my hand and twists my arm behind me, jerking me to his chest.

"Do not attempt a struggle, wench, for I would snap thy bone in two as soon as I would kiss thee." His foul breath is hot beside my ear. "Rank and privilege be damned; beneath, we are man and woman. This night, in this chamber, I will prove that to you."

Awareness whirls, and anger boils! The fiend's grip does not falter as his free hand presses 'gainst my hip. I pray to the saints above, and to my mother, for assistance.

Barnardo pulls me round to face him; his hand slithers upward to cup my breast. I near convulse at his touch, giving forth a shudder of true disgust. He laughs, mistaking my repugnance for passion.

"Ah, the *lady* likes this! You see, how like a whore a lady is when Barnardo handles her? You want this, Ophelia, do not make to disclaim it."

Through a haze of rage, I glimpse the row of pots along my window ledge.

Inspiration!

At once, I effect an expression of utter coyness, and will the fury from my voice to speak. "A drink, sir?"

"What?" Waylaid, Barnardo flinches, drawing back to study my eyes.

I lower my lashes. "You are true, good Barnardo. I confess, I have oft looked hungrily upon thee, thinking thoughts most intimate. You have discovered me, and now we are free to bring those thoughts to action."

He blinks, as beads of perspiration glisten on his brow. "What?"

"A drink," I whisper. "A toast to us, together at last." I go up on tiptoe to place a small kiss upon his throat, ignoring the odious taste of his skin. His grip upon me falters; he clings lightly now, as I lead him to the ledge.

Barnardo gulps. "Wine. Aye."

"Wine and then some," I say in a husky giggle, seductive and contrived, as I run my fingers gracefully up a slim stem of dogbane, an herb sometimes called bitterroot.

"This night calls for something mystical, a secret nectar. Now, pour the wine, sir, whilst I prepare the potion."

"Potion?" His eyes narrow, not with distrust but with interest. "Pray tell, vixen, what manner of manly talent dost thou crave which this tonic might provide?"

I bring my lips close to his ear and whisper a promise so salacious I can actually feel his pulse quicken. I repeat the order. "Pour the wine."

He does so, trembling. The tide has shifted; prisoner am I no longer. It frightens him, nay, terrifies him, to imagine that what he thought to take will be so freely given. I've drained him of all power in this position—and soon I will drain him of much else!

He hands me my goblet and his. I've no time to calculate the amount of dogbane required for his size, and so I overcompensate with a fat handful of blooms, several seeds from one plump pod, and a great milky drop of the stem's thick juice.

He watches as each ingredient sends ripples 'cross the cup.

"Drink, sir, and lustily." I stroke his cheek. "Though I am certain you need no assistance in romantic matters, I believe we both have much to gain from the gifts of this potion."

He hurries the chalice to his mouth to guzzle the well-laced wine, gulping it down his gullet. I sip mine daintily.

For a moment, he waits, a look of wondrous expectancy on his face. I chew my lower lip, afeared mayhap the malicious mixture be too slight for this monster's considerable girth.

"Anything, sir?" I venture.

Barnardo tilts his head in thought. And then a most unpleasant rumble thunders forth from his midsection.

The idiot smiles. "Ah . . . something. Something indeed!" His eyes gleam. "Ready thyself, wench, to be astonished and grateful."

I cannot suppress the yelp of dread as his lips come down to mine. And then an even greater rumble. The kiss becomes a moan.

He growls. "God's teeth!"

"Sir?"

"I fear your potion hath faulty aim. It's not gone far south enough to cast its spell! Dear God, the magic has sorely missed its mark."

"No, Barnardo," I assure him. "It has made a direct hit!"

Again he groans. His skin, I note, is a most offensive green in color.

"You . . . devious . . . wench!"

"I shall once more remind you, cur, that is not how one addresses a lady!"

Using the heat of all my hatred, I fold a fist and land it hard upon his jaw. He staggers backward, the polluted wine sloshing from his cup. "That one is for me," I tell him. "And this"—with every ounce of strength I possess, I direct my knee into the spot he described as south of his stomach— "is for Anne!"

He is breathless a moment, then a most repulsive sound hammers through my chamber as the heaving commences.

Grinning, I call o'er my shoulder, as I leave him there to sully the rushes with his retching:

*"A feminine mind hath kept thy male body from its most ignoble goal.*
*Would that with your supper there, you'd spew forth your tainted soul!"*

# CHAPTER SEVEN

MY FATHER'S HOUSE AWAITS ME, WARMLY. I HAVE
run all the way from Elsinore.

"Ophelia, child! What is the matter?"

I stumble inside to be caught in his embrace.

"Father . . . the play. Oh, Father, the play . . ."

"There, now," he whispers, leading me to a seat beside
the hearth. "Catch your breath, and tell me what has happened."

Around us wafts the liquid scent of herbs well steeped.
I brush the snow from my skirts, kick off my damp shoes.
"Hamlet hath proven Claudius guilty of the murder of the
King."

"At the play?"

"Through the play," I clarify. "With the play. *In* the
play. Hamlet adjusted the plot so that it was, in fact, a
re-enactment of Claudius's crime."

"Clever lad."

"Yes, for, at the sight of it, Claudius did fly into a most turbid fit! Evidence of his culpability, surely! I would have gone after him, as Hamlet did, but Horatio did worry for my safety. He ordered, in good faith, a guard, Barnardo, to attend me to mine chamber! By the blood of Saint Ermengild, I have never before feared the presence of a man, but tonight . . ."

His eyes go dark with worry. "Did the brute harm thee, daughter?"

"Nearly, but I sallied his scheme!" The memory sets a queer feeling of pride and repulsion tumbling in my belly. "I sensed his aim was not to seduce but to overpower me."

"Aye, men of that ilk are often so inclined. What did you do?"

"I made to enjoy it, Father, pretending that his attentions did excite me. It confounded him, the witless dolt, to be removed of his might. Frightened him as well, I do believe."

My father approves. "When a woman is without a dirk, she is fortunate to have intellect as a weapon." He strokes my rumpled hair. "What then?"

"I fed him dogbane, sir."

"Dogbane!" At this, a most appreciative laugh! "Zounds, child, you'll return to find fouled rushes for certain."

"A small price, Father." I clear my throat and go on with my confession. "And then I slugged him. In the jaw, to begin, and followed with a knee to his . . ."

"So you pummeled the cur, besides! Ho! I have here a quite resourceful girl."

The laughter rings louder as mine mingles with his. "It is most satisfying for a daughter to so please her father."

His laughter trails off. We are silent a moment; he reaches for a horn cup, pours some herb-scented liquid, and hands the drink to me. I sip gratefully. The concoction is warm, with a leafy-sweet sting. He waits till I have finished the cup.

"Pray thee, child," he asks in a solemn voice, "what now?"

"I must speak to Hamlet. We shall confer, to determine a course. He will surely kill the King, and quickly, now that his guilt has been availed!"

"Lia!"

We whirl, my father and I, to find Anne in the doorway, shivering.

My father is up and bundling her inside. He pours some of the hot liquid into a second vessel and gives it to Anne. For a moment, she but stares at him.

"Anne," I say softly, "my father."

She does not think to question it—rather, drops a small curtsy, still trembling. My father guides her to the seat that was his, then brings a shawl for her shoulders.

A look of concern tightens her face. "I saw you spirited off by Barnardo after the King's wild exit from the play."

"Not to worry, friend, as I am well."

"Saints be praised, then." She sighs, crossing herself. "For you may be the only one!"

"How did you find me?" I ask, falling to my knees to remove her sodden slippers. I notice that most of her skirt is soaked through and her right leg is wet to the knee.

"'Twas a task, that!" she assures me. "I thought first to try the stream, as you oft go there to ruminate. I tripped thrice over snow-covered stones on the way, and did not realize I'd reached the pool until I'd put my foot through the thin ice that covered it! Lucky I am that the moon be bright this night, else I would ne'er have seen your tracks in the snow on the opposite side. I leapt across, and followed the trail." She pauses to sip from the cup, then slants a questioning glance at my father.

"Speak freely," I tell her. "He knows all."

Anne closes her eyes. "So much, in so short a span, hath happened!"

"Hamlet—is he hurt?"

"No. But he is in greatest danger."

"How do you know?" my father asks, taking her empty cup to fill it yet again.

"I followed him from the moment he left the play in pursuit of Claudius. At first I could not decide whether to go after you, Lia, should you need me in defense against Barnardo. But as you are more capable than most of taking care of yourself, I determined I would better serve thee by gathering information. So off I went, on Hamlet's heels."

She inhales, a long shuddering breath. "I had all I could do to keep sight of him in the fray. He went first to Horatio, then led him to a private place, out of doors. The south quadrangle. And there, as I concealed myself in the shadow of the broad door, Hamlet explained to Horatio that he did now believe the ghost's word. Not a moment later, his old friends discovered them. You remember, Lia—the teeth, the curls?"

"That would be Rosencrantz and Guildenstern. Yes, Anne. I remember."

"They bid Hamlet go to his mother, saying that his behavior had struck her into amazement."

"Did he go?"

"Not straightaway. In fact, he lingered with his fellows, playing mad, beseeching one to play upon a pipe. I listened from the shadows, and then Horatio caught sight of me. I called upon all courage and crooked my finger at him."

This surprises me, and for a moment I forget the dire nature of her tale. "You crooked your finger at Horatio?" I actually smile. "How flirtatious, Anne."

"It was hardly flirtation, Lia. 'Twas desperation, nothing more."

"Still, 'twas bold! I'm proud of you."

"I told Horatio my plan to follow the Prince in order that I might bring all news to thee. His eyes did dance with approval as he praised the breadth of my bravery, called me a most loyal and—dare I repeat it?—*lovely* friend."

"Methinks good Horatio partook of some flirtation of his own."

Anne flushes clear to her shoulders. "He did then a most remarkable thing! He pulled from his boot a small dagger—which he gave to me, saying, 'Take this to protect thyself, for suddenly I find that I would be inconsolable should any harm come to thee.'"

"This Horatio," my father observes, "seems a smooth one."

"Smooth, perhaps, but genuine," I tell Anne. "I am sure of it!"

Again, she blushes. "When the dagger was safely in my sleeve, he touched my cheek, then went back to the hall to attempt to calm the ruckus. No sooner did he go than your father—that is, your *other* father—which is to say, the one who *was* your father, but never *really*—"

"Yes, yes. Polonius. We know to whom you refer."

"Polonius, yes." She nods, struggling to retain her logic. "Polonius appeared, also to summon Hamlet to the Queen. Here, now, I found a problem. I felt it crucial for me to hear the Prince's discourse with the Queen, but, were I to attempt to follow him to Gertrude's chamber, I would surely be noticed. Can you guess what I did?"

"Well, I know that you are a most clever and resourceful girl, and so my guess is that you hastened to the hidden door—the one Laertes revealed to us as children, the one which opens on a little-known passageway leading directly to the Queen's sitting room."

I pause to recollect how, when Anne and I were very

young, we'd make mischievous use of that tunnel, secreting ourselves into Gertrude's room and playing dress up in her jewels and gowns! "I remember it thick with cobwebs."

"They are still there!" snaps Anne, swiping at the sticky remains of one that clings to her hair. "But, yes! I bested Hamlet by several minutes, taking that shortcut. I arrived at Gertrude's chamber the same moment as Polonius, who made his entrance properly through the door. Gertrude was pacing, wringing her hands and crying out, holding first her head and then her heart. With Polonius focused on her antics, I was able to slip into the room and quickly conceal myself behind the large woven tapestry that hangs on the broadest wall."

"A perfect hiding spot."

"Hah!" Anne lets out a snort. "I thought so too, at the time. You will see presently that it was nearly the end of me."

My eyes go round. "Go on!"

"From my place of concealment, I listened as Polonius urged Gertrude to chastise the Prince for his pranks. We heard Hamlet approaching, and next I knew—there was Polonius, beside me behind the arras!"

"Dear God! What did he do?"

"Nothing. The old fool was so stunned to find me there, he merely gaped. This gave me opportunity to withdraw Horatio's dagger and hold it to his throat. I did not need to tell him my purpose; he knew that if he uttered but a single sound I would slit his throat."

"Anne! How positively heroic!"

"Not at all like me," she admits. "But the circumstance allowed none other." She pauses to sip from the cup. "Hamlet stormed in then, in a most indescribable state. His voice was heavy with hatred, disappointment, dread! Such a screaming scolding did he hurl against his Queen, her terror almost tangible, reaching us even behind the weighty cover of the arras! Through a small hole worn in the fabric of the tapestry, I saw her reach out her arms in an overture of motherly comfort. But Hamlet shoved away her embrace, causing her to topple backward on the bed. And then, in mortal fear, she did cry out, 'Help, ho!' Polonius lost his composure and echoed her shout with a shout of his own! Hamlet, convinced, I am sure, that the voice was Claudius's, withdrew his rapier and, with instinctive accuracy, drove it through the arras into the heart of his hidden prey."

"Hell's teeth, Anne, you were standing right beside him!"

She shakes her head at the memory. "Had his aim been less than true, I might be telling this tale to you dead!"

"What then?"

"Polonius fell. Slid, actually, down the wall and out from under, so that his legs were visible from the other side. Hamlet grabbed him at the ankles and yanked, causing only the faintest ripple of the tapestry, thus not unveiling me as I stood there frozen, still holding Horatio's dagger poised in the spot where Polonius's throat had been."

"And what said Hamlet when he found 'twas not the King he murdered?"

"Well, he called the deceased a rash, intruding fool, but there was deep remorse in his tone. I do not believe that Prince Hamlet is overly fond of murder."

"How did the Queen react?"

"There was a good deal more crying and pleading as Hamlet continued his brutal reprimand. It was a most unpleasant scene, Hamlet ranting, Gertrude writhing! I felt terribly impolite witnessing it, and of course there was Polonius's blood pooling at my feet. . . . I daresay, I was almost relieved when the ghost arrived!"

My father's eyes widen in shock. "Ghost?"

Anne nods and replies in a casual tone, "The ghost of Hamlet's father."

"Ah," says my father weakly. "That ghost."

Eagerly, I inquire: "Did Gertrude see the apparition?"

"Nay, she did not. Or, at least, she said she did not. When Hamlet addressed the specter, she seemed certain more than ever of his madness. The ghost reminded Hamlet that his purpose was not to bully his mother but, rather, to avenge his father. When the ghost departed, Hamlet's mien was far less violent; they talked of his packing off to England."

My soul does lurch within me. I had nearly forgotten! England!

"I waited," Anne concludes, "until Hamlet lugged the

guts of Polonius away. In his absence, Gertrude dissolved into tears, providing me a safe egress to the secret door."

"You did not continue after Hamlet?" I ask.

"Not directly. I discovered in our passage a second passage, winding off to the left, which I took, and through which I found myself lost and wandering in darkness for near an hour! Time enough, I would soon learn, for the King to hear of Polonius's unnatural demise. When at last I saw light, I headed for it. It was a small grate near the ceiling of a room from which came voices—Claudius's and Hamlet's. Claudius was demanding the whereabouts of Polonius's body, and Hamlet was being exceptionally cagey, telling nothing. He was, in fact, rather funny!"

For a moment Anne smiles, but then her eyes go cold, her mouth sets in a serious line. "He told where the corpse was stashed, and then the conversation turned abruptly to the subject of his immediate departure for England."

"Immediate?" My head bows of its own accord, as a most profound loneliness begins to pound within me. "He has gone already?"

"Aye," whispers Anne.

Gone. He is gone.

Without the vindication of revenge, without so much as a kiss from me. Oh, we had not the time to discuss his exile—or how or if he would return! He, there; I, here—an eternity of ocean between us, and no hope at all to bridge it. Unless . . .

"I must go!"

"Go?" repeat my friend and father as one.

"To England!"

Yes! I leap to my feet, enthusiasm building with every fervent step I take round the small cottage.

"I shall sail for England by myself at the earliest occasion. I will secure passage on another ship bound for that destination, and once on English soil, it will be nothing to find Hamlet."

"It will be too late," says Anne, her voice alarmingly flat.

"What do you mean, too late?"

"He will be dead, Lia, before you even reach English waters."

Dead? I shiver . . . try to speak . . . cannot.

Tears bloom in Anne's eyes. "Claudius has decreed it, ordered it in letters sealed and sent along with Hamlet, in the hands of his escorts. He has charged England by royal command to see to the death of Hamlet. 'Do it, England,' those were Claudius's own and ugly words. He sends Hamlet there to face his execution. And, Lia, even upon the swiftest ship, even in the chariot of Apollo himself, you nor anyone would arrive in time to save him. By the devil's pointy tail, Lia, Claudius in his iniquity has won. Again."

Hamlet.

Dead?

Before my tears begin in earnest, I manage this: "Oh, but he has *not* won, Anne. For he has not yet fought with *me!*"

And now I hear a wailing sound—a bellow, a cry, a

roar—and am remotely aware that the sound escapes from me. The wail fades to weeping. I am in my father's arms, and Anne's, and the night goes on in a slow, cold current around me.

*Allow me but one night to weep, then alone shall I avenge the crown*
*But God, dear God, the tide of this despair is deep. Do not let me*
*drown.*

# CHAPTER EIGHT

I SEND WORD TO MY BROTHER.

Anne delivers my letter to Horatio this very night, asking that he forward it to France.

From the doorway, I watch as she sets out across the darkness. So black a night I've never seen, nor felt, as I feel this one in my heart.

My father gives me more steeped herbs, and I fall into an almost-slumber, shivering and racked with the memory of my loss.

ँ ँ ँ

In the icy light of dawn, I return to the castle Elsinore. There is a stench in my room; the chamber all but echoes with Barnardo's retching. I send for a maid to replace the rushes, and notice that she eyes me cautiously as she cleans. I know why. Anne has begun the rumor. She has whispered among the servants that since last night I have been afflicted with a most peculiar manner.

At noon, I hide on the stairs to overhear the conversation at dinner. As expected, the courtiers discuss my condition at great lengths. None will dispute it. My father killed at the hand of my love, my love banished to a foreign land—naturally I've gone mad!

It is all, of course, merely the continuation of the plan contrived for Hamlet.

Hamlet who is gone to England to be killed.

The pain, the grief, consumes me—an ache so thorough, an agony so severe! Mayhap madness *will* come for me like a wave crashing o'er the fathomless flood of dread emotion to pull me under, carry me away.

I cannot say that I would mind it. Anything to elude this misery.

Oh, to have stayed before the crackling fire upon the hearth within my father's cottage. But I have resigned myself to live in the gloom of Elsinore until the business of destroying Claudius is done. While I hate with all my heart each particle of sediment in every stone of this castle, I cannot leave here yet. I must stalk the fiend and do so closely. Claudius is the villain, yet it is I who am in prison. Only Anne and my garden are left to comfort me.

Yet I wish to remember as much as to forget, and so, on a parchment scroll, I set to work painstakingly recording the details of Claudius's wicked deed. Who knows how long 'twill be before I may officially accuse him before a court of justice? I would have nothing o'erlooked. As well, there is the possibility that some ungodly violence could occur—some danger visited upon me, inflicted perhaps by a vindictive Barnardo, or the King himself, should he suspect. And so I write.

I would much rather slit the King's throat but will not do this for two reasons. One, it is a sin. Two, I do not own a sharp enough knife.

There is a knock on my door; Anne enters.

"Since you did not come to dinner, I have brought you . . ."

Before she can set the trencher down, a shadow falls across the floor. I look to see Claudius in my doorway. Anne takes a step backward. I simply stare, too shocked by this unusual and ill-timed visit even to think to conceal the written denunciation before me.

"Lovely Ophelia," he begins, approaching me. "I wish to offer thee condolences on the death of your honored father."

He takes my hand to kiss, slivers of something sordid in his eyes, and I realize of a sudden the damning parchment is in plain sight! My only hope is to divert him, and so I answer:

"My father, sir, is alive. I saw him but an hour past."

A flicker of something—is it pleasure?—contorts the forged King's face. Ah, so he has come to test the allegations of my madness; I do believe he hopes to find them true!

"He was here?" challenges the King. "Polonius? Alive!"

"Alive enough to borrow my russet gown." I giggle. "'Tis a poor color on him, and it makes him appear plump round the middle. But 'tis his favorite."

"Your father," he stammers, "wore your gown?"

He turns to Anne for confirmation. She effects a look of great pity, shaking her head.

"Polonius dons my garments often," I assure the King. "But shhh! He prefers that no one know of it, sire. He would beat me if I told. I am also to keep secret the fact that he can fly."

At this nonsense he is truly aghast. "Say you, Ophelia, that Polonius flies? That is to say, he makes himself airborne?"

"Aye, my lord. Airborne. Like a stallion."

"But stallions cannot fly, lady."

"Perhaps not those with whom you are acquainted, sire."

Claudius blinks, confounded.

"And now," I say blithely, "I must rest." With that, I drop to my pallet and commence to snore.

"What make thee of this?" Claudius barks, shaking his finger at Anne.

She glances down at me, then shrugs. "She is tired."

"No!" booms Claudius. "What make thee of her madness?!"

"She's lost her father, sire," says Anne, in a respectful tone. "I expect it has driven her to an unbalanced state."

"Will it last?"

"That is hard to say, my lord. Madness has been known to linger."

For a moment, the King stands mutely by my bed; I feel him staring down at me.

Then there comes the sound of his footsteps, the slam of the door, and Anne's great sigh.

"Old Polonius in your gown!" She plants her hands on her hips. "I believe the King to be sufficiently convinced."

"Aye. The unfortunate thing now is that, following flying stallions, I will need work very hard to maintain such a level of insanity!"

Anne rolls her eyes. "You are surely up to it."

I want so to laugh at her expression. But there is no laughter left within me.

And it, like Hamlet, is not likely to return.

# CHAPTER NINE

THE NIGHTS AT ELSINORE ARE LONGER THAN ANY-
where else.

I have stayed awake these many weeks, which has aided
me greatly in my portrayal of one who has gone daft. For
my skin is pale as fresh daisy petals, and my eyes sink
inward, rimmed by bruiselike swells of purple. The servants and courtiers whisper that, surely, Ophelia—*most
beautified Ophelia*—has lost touch.

I sleep not, which is nothing new, though in days past
'twas joy or wonder kept me up. But this is wakefulness
born of fear. Who will come for me should I close my eyes
to sleep—*to sleep, perchance to dream . . .* ? What criminal hand
will curl round my throat while I doze, defenseless and
unaware? Or, worse, will bring to me its chill, unwanted
caress?

Of late, the King has taken to imposing his presence upon me. He corners me in the chapel, or stops me on the stairs, and makes intimate advances, which cause my skin to crawl. I fear the day draws nigh when he will realize his licentious purpose.

'Tis winter's end. Constellations shift, and earth's frosty crust commences to thaw, yet still no sign of Laertes. In daylight, I gather buds of unborn blossoms and visit with my father, where I am allowed a brief respite. But at Elsinore, I make the most inappropriate remarks to the Queen and dance as a wanton might, often upon the table at supper.

Barnardo perceives such performances with great interest; at night, I bolt the door.

And still I do not sleep.

I have counted every crack in the ashlar stones that make my walls and have listened to the manic music of mice fighting in far corners of the chamber and have burned things just for the company of smoke.

But I do not sleep. Sleep is spent, and what remains is something numb and wasted within me. In the place where rest once was, there is only longing, a yearning that slumber cannot overcome.

I call out to Hamlet and dream with eyes wide open of shared kisses and *words, words, words.* . . .

Once, I held a dagger to my wrist and counted to eight thousand and six.

No. Be gone! The madness sweeps down, a foul fairy, wielding a wand carved of bone and dressed in rags dyed with blood. I swat at it, and spit, and the fairy gets tangled in my hair.

My hair, how Hamlet loved to wrap his fingers in it! Dirty now, flat and slick against my scalp. Anne begs to wash it. But why? The fairy will just come again and . . .

No. Be gone!

I make to the shelf and lose myself in the herbs there, pushing back the madness, whose dearest friend is fatigue—pressing my nose into the blooms of something sweet. Restore me! Let me breathe in the perfect purity of that which springs from good rich soil. And name it!

Goldenrod and juniper!

Jack-in-the-pulpit.

Ginseng, Solomon's seal.

And nettles! Nettles, with their toothed leaves and prickly hairs—see you how they bristle up from the stem, see you, Hamlet?

Hamlet . . . look, there's rosemary for remembrance, and pansies, that's for thoughts.

No! 'Tis an ugly dream that comes without the benefit of sleep! Damn the sport of madness that forgets itself! I am not mad. Will not *be* mad.

Deep breath. Small sigh. I call upon the moon to mother me, but of late she has been still. No longer can she bear to share with me her silvery secrets, offer counsel or caution, as she did when Hamlet lived.

I must shake off this state that tempts me—for there is no freedom in true madness.

Only freedom in the game of it.

Deep breath, a prayer.

I am tired, only tired.

From somewhere near to heaven, arms encircle me. Soft. Gentle. And a song, sung in a voice like breeze and rain. I drop my head back and find it resting on first a shoulder, unseen . . . now a pillow—I have come, somehow, to lay upon my bed.

The arms hold me still, and the lullaby is a whisper, coaxing me to sleep, to close my eyes.

*"Sleep, Ophelia."*

She sings. And I sleep.

Oh, at last, I sleep.

In a heartbeat, it is morning.

## CHAPTER TEN

A FORTNIGHT, PERHAPS TWO. SPRING HAS KEPT ITS promise in a froth of buds upon the branches.

'Tis twilight, and the air is powder soft. Anne and I are walking near the stables, for I do so miss the horses. (I am not allowed to ride, as I am feeble-minded now.) The rhythm of their switching tails, the familiar sound of a satisfied whinny, the faint smell of hay and leather provide solace to my heart.

"For you," I say to Anne, gifting her with a sprig of delicate white flowers.

"Pretty."

"'Tis called yarrow. The healthy blooms signify love eternal."

"I will be sure to show Horatio." She brushes the flowers against her palm. "He worries greatly after thee, you know, as a brother would. Are you certain we cannot confide in him?"

"'Twould be at his own peril," I remind her. "Any who knows of our deceit becomes the instantaneous enemy of the King. 'Twas different when he conspired with Hamlet, for that was expected. Now his distance is his deliverance."

Anne frowns. "I do not wish to endanger him."

"Of course you don't. He is well to be removed from this, Anne. Trust me."

"'Tis a hazardous game we're about," she agrees. "And you are right; I rest easier knowing he is not a part of it."

"I am moved to know he cares, though. Perhaps, one day, I will be able to thank him for his concern."

Anne tucks the yarrow sprig behind her ear, then enters the stable; she has promised the stablemaster's son to bring sugar for a mare who is soon to foal.

The moon is rising slowly; it is not yet full dark. Something about the hour troubles me, this not-quite-one-still-not-another space where darkness hovers, threatening. I shiver and call to Anne.

"We should go back . . . ," I begin. But a hand across my mouth stops me.

"Pretty Ophelia."

The voice comes thickly, and with it the stink of ale. The body pressed to mine is too soft to be Barnardo's.

Claudius!

"I have daily thanked heaven for this plague that has o'ertaken thee. For now I can do as I wish—as long I've dreamed to do! Do you know, lady, how I would seethe with jealousy when I'd watch my nephew close to thee, knowing that in private he was free to savor the perfections of your youth. No doubt the blackhearted boy's deprived me of your maidenly virtue."

He removes his hand to grab at the bodice of my gown; he tears it away, then does the same to the slender straps of my silk chemise, until I am revealed to him in the moonlight.

The demon's eyes glint, like the fires of hell.

"In madness, thou art still beautiful, and better—for accusations made in madness are not to be believed!"

I cross my arms to cover myself but can seem to do naught else. I will my legs to run, my throat to scream, but neither happens. I recoil in anticipation of his touch. But no touch comes.

"Just a glimpse is wanted now," he hisses, "as I shall make this process long and slow. Each day, a slight, sweet torture upon myself I shall inflict, to whet my need, until at last—"

A noise. He spins to see a shadow rounding the corner of the stable, armed with a pitchfork.

"I will come for thee," he swears, then vanishes into the gathering darkness, his footsteps slapping in the muddy earth.

"Lia!"

I fall to my knees in the muck. Anne drops the pitchfork, hurries to remove her cloak, and bundles it round me.

"I did not fight," I whisper, the taste of shame and

disbelief bitter on my tongue. "Why, Anne, could I not fight?"

"You were wise not to resist," she tells me. "You are weak from lack of rest and too much grief. Who knows how he would have harmed thee!"

"And next time . . . will I be too frail then, as well?"

Anne looks at me; she has no answer.

"I would sooner die than have Claudius touch me, Anne! Yet the offense of his intention is so powerful that I am helpless to defend against it."

Anne assists me to my feet, and we head slowly toward the castle. "What wilt thou do?" she inquires in a whisper.

"'Tis simple," I say softly. "I must die."

ॐ ॐ ॐ

At dawn, I hear the clatter of hooves, a commotion below in the bailey.

A guard's voice thunders on the mild air to reach my room: "What, ho! 'Tis Laertes, returned from France!"

Laertes! Merciful saints, praise thee for seeing to his safe passage! I rush to the window and see him reining to a halt, congenially accosted by his fellows!

"How do you, Laertes? How fared thee, in France?"

"Give news of the women there! 'Tis true that they . . . ?"

"Soft, fellows," scolds one. "Dost thou forget he comes home to mourn his father?"

"Aye, and the lady Ophelia."

Laertes dismounts; flinging the reins to his groom, he whirls to take hold of him who's mentioned me.

"What of my sister?" he demands. "Why dost thou speak her name in so grave a tone?"

Horatio steps in to drag my brother aside. "Restrain thyself, friend, I beseech thee. Grim revelations are imminent, which will require on your part much strength to endure."

A wave from Horatio causes all but Laertes' groom to disperse. When they are alone, Laertes takes Horatio by the shoulders and meets his eyes with a look of greatest desperation.

"Tell me, Horatio. A missive came to me in France to report the passing of my father! 'Tis true?"

"Regretfully do I confirm it, friend. Polonius is dead."

My brother crosses himself. "Pray, what illness befell him?"

"One that was not his. 'Twas the diseased condition of another that brought about the death of the old man."

Even from this distance, I see the cold gleam of comprehension in Laertes' eye. "Murdered! Dear God, then what is there to tell of my sister? Never say this tragedy be twofold!"

Horatio lowers his head. "'Tis tragic, aye, but—"

"I need only know this," Laertes interrupts. "Is she alive?"

Horatio nods.

"Then I shall first to the cemetery to pay my father his final respect. I will see to Ophelia anon." With a hand-up from his groom, he once more gains his mount and speaks from the saddle with chilling calm. "I am full ready to avenge this crime, and I believe I know on whom to place the blame. Warn Claudius if you must." His brow beads with the heat of his defiance. "But mark me—an entire legion of Swiss guards surrounding him is not sufficient protection from the sword of this wronged son."

Horatio says naught for a long moment. Surely he will not betray the Prince by telling Laertes 'twas Hamlet, not Claudius, who killed Polonius!

"I am no great admirer of this King, Laertes. He will not learn from me that you are here. Nor will anyone else. And I shall instruct those who have already welcomed you to keep silent on't as well. I am confident they will oblige, as they are most excellent friends of yours."

Laertes nods his gratitude. "'Tis not difficult to see why my sister did always speak highly of thee."

"Did she?" A smile brightens Horatio's handsome face. "In days past, that news would have made my heart spin circles."

"'Tis no longer the case?" Laertes cocks an eyebrow. "Not even with Hamlet gone?"

"It has been months since I've thought upon your sister amorously. In your absence, in fact, I have come to feel intensely protective toward her."

Laertes grins. "There is another, then? Shall I guess who? The lovely Anne?"

I would not have believed it possible, but Horatio actually flushes.

"Little Anne! When we were children, I put spiders down her dress."

"I would advise thee not to try it now, or you will answer to me for being too close!"

Laertes throws his head back and laughs!

Horatio heaves a sigh, and now his eyes turn solemn. "As much as I enjoy sharing kind humor with thee, friend, I am ashamed to do so. For, even as we speak, your sister—"

Laertes flicks the reins to cut him short. "Hold, Horatio. Not now. I will contend with whatever is her lamentable circumstance once I've said a proper farewell to my slain father. And then I will gather numbers who await me in the countryside—men I have already enlisted to support me in my cause. You see, your news of murder stung but did not surprise me. I suspected such treachery and came prepared."

Horatio nods. "Godspeed."

With a shout, Laertes spurs his steed and is off.

🍂 🍂 🍂

I find him at the stream and call from a distance.

"Ho, there. Be thou my brother?"

A cautious glance. "You know I am."

I rush to him, waving the bouquet I've brought along, then stop short. He stares at me a moment, taking in my poor appearance.

"No," I say, with a jerking motion of my head. "For my

brother is the glorious Laertes. King of the Dragonflies. Hast thou seen him?"

His mouth falls open.

I spin a circle, then hop twice, then bow. "Shall I sing for you, stranger? Indeed! I shall.

> *"I see a maiden, all in white,*
> *Ha-loo, ha-loo, and diddle down,*
> *A maiden chaste and pure and right,*
> *A-diddle down, ha-loo,*
> *I ask her why she waits alone,*
> *Ha-loo, ha-loo, and diddle dee,*
> *She says, for one she once has known,*
> *Young he was, but now he's grown,*
> *Whose sword is sharp within its sheath.*
> *Her gown has nothing underneath,*
> *Diddle down, ha-loo!"*

I stop, a hair's breadth from him, and gaze wild-eyed into his face. A moment passes, and then:

"Sprite!" He lifts me off my feet and spins me round, laughing. "Awful girl! I near believed your madness real! And where, pray, did you learn such bawdy songs?"

"From thee, brother! Those randy rhymes you did recite to me when you were but a boy! Remember how you and Hamlet would dare me to repeat them to my nurse?"

"I do."

"And if I am awful," I say, smacking at him with my

bouquet, "you are equally so. Your performance for Horatio was quite commendable! One would never guess I'd told you all in my letter!" I sigh. "'Twas a moment there I thought he might disappoint me. I feared he would tell thee the truth of who murdered Polonius. But his loyalty holds, even subsequent to Hamlet's death. I am glad and touched to know it."

Now Laertes falls to close examination of my person, frowning with concern. "You are thinner, girl, unpleasingly so. And the color I recall so fondly upon your cheeks is fiercely lacking. And your hair . . . heaven save me, child, what have you done to your hair?"

"Nothing, and that is the problem. I have not washed, nor combed, nor plaited it in—oh, I forget how long!"

"Horrific!"

"That was my intention."

"Then you have succeeded, verily. I have longed to talk to thee."

Dropping happily to the grass, I pull upon his sleeve till he joins me. A grin tugs at the corner of his mouth as his glance falls upon the bundle of herbs and flowers I grasp.

"Still busy with your weeds, I see."

"Aye. Perfume or poison, take your pick."

"Well, I had quite enough of perfume while in France," says he. "The women there are quite liberal with it, as well as with their charms."

"Adored you, did they?" I effect a look of disapproval.

"They did." The sparkle in his eyes fades suddenly. "Alas, there are issues more important to discuss. I would know what designs you have toward bringing Claudius to justice. Were Hamlet here, revenge would be the only road—indeed, the rightful one. But for you or me or anyone else to slay him—even in his guilt—would be naught more than murder."

"Aye." I let out a long rush of breath. "There's the rub."

"Hamlet," he repeats, taking my hand. "You must miss him sorely."

"You cannot imagine."

How I would so love to curl up in the grass, head upon Laertes' knee, and bask in the romance of his tales from afar. But I've much to tell him—of the poison I've brewed and its peculiar properties, of last night's brush with the satyr who is King, and the means by which I shall escape him.

'Twill be a long explanation. I begin it by handing Laertes the small vial which contains the magic of my scheme.

## CHAPTER ELEVEN

"Where is the beauteous Majesty of Denmark?"

I tiptoe into the hall, looking verily disturbed. My filthy hair is strewn with dead flowers, and I have smudged my nose with dirt. My gown I wear with its back in front; the coarseness of the stone floor bites the soles of my bare feet.

Gertrude trembles as I make across the space in her direction, first skipping, then stomping, then again on tiptoe. Horatio stands beside her. (Moments ago, Anne reported that he'd gone to seek out the Queen for the purpose of begging her to speak with me.)

"How now, Ophelia?" asks the Queen most nervously. In answer, I begin to sing.

> *"He is dead and gone, lady,*
> *He is dead and gone;*

*At his head a grass-green turf,*
*At his heels a stone.*

"Oh, ho!"

She makes to interrupt, but again I demand she listen, scampering away to avoid her outstretched arms. 'Tis pity she offers? Or comfort? God's truth, should she attempt to soothe me, I know not what I'd do. For I did love her once! 'Twas her motherly hands which softly stroked my forehead on the day my mother died. And Hamlet! How certain we both were that she taught the stars to shine! But to forgive her now?

The Queen's ladies whisper their horror as I twirl and gallop and chant. Horatio waves them out; as they take their leave, the King appears. Upon spying me, he halts his stride and makes no other move.

I pause before him, meet him toe to toe, and fire a hateful look at him.

He flinches! Aye, and flinch he should, for what he's done to me. Perhaps now he fears my unruly condition. His voice is tremulous when he inquires, "How do you, pretty lady?"

I bare my teeth and bark at him. He steps backward in alarm, and I grin, calming my demeanor to speak nonsense.

"They say the owl was a baker's daughter." I thrust myself toward him, so that my nose near meets his chin, and change my light tone to loathing. "Lord, we know what we are, but know not what we may be!"

*And what you are,* I am thinking, *is a heathen swine, who made the grave mistake of wronging me!*

The color drains from his face. I smile, tilt my head in a careless gesture, and finish sweetly, "God be at your table!"

Gathering up my skirts, I dance away, humming, giggling, and wailing in turn. I slow my pace when I reach Horatio; I reach out a sisterly hand and touch his cheek, hoping somehow he will see beyond this make-believe and know that I am well.

The Queen arrives at the King's side. He presumes aloud that I am thinking of my father. His erroneous judgment angers me—does it not occur to him that it is the loss of Hamlet, and not the soulless simpkin Polonius, which torments me? I drop to the floor and slither toward them as a serpent. The Queen shrieks and covers her face, while the King makes to shield himself behind her.

I roll a somersault and spring to my feet. "Pray you, let's have no words of this," I hiss, "but when they ask you what it means, say you this:

> *"Tomorrow is Saint Valentine's day,*
> *All in the morning betime,*
> *And I a maid at your window,*
> *To be your Valentine.*

*Then up he rose, and donned his clothes,*
*And dupped the chamber door;*
*Let in the maid, that out a maid*
*Never departed more."*

"Pretty Ophelia—"

Damn, but I wish he'd stop calling me that! I cram myself between the King and Queen to drape my arm companionably round her shoulder, as though we were lads just finished downing tankards of ale, and sing a bawdy rhyme.

"How long has she been thus?" the King asks.

Before the Queen can answer, I wriggle out of the space, turn, and make a deep, deep curtsy.

"I hope all will be well," I whisper, then adopt a cheery tone as I beckon an invisible entourage. "Good night, ladies; good night, sweet ladies; good night, good night." Bowing and waving, I take my leave of them.

Anne is waiting without, eyes wide with amazement.

"Well?" I prompt.

"I best liked the slithering part!"

I pull a moldy stem from my hair and giggle. "Thank you, I quite agree."

"Soft, Horatio comes!"

"Ladies . . ."

"That is a matter of opinion," I coo, spinning a small pirouette.

Anne gives me a quelling look. Horatio positions himself between us; with his back to me, he speaks in a low voice.

"The King suggests I keep an eye on her," Horatio tells Anne. "What think you?" She looks o'er his shoulder for a clue from me. I shake my head.

"Let me," she tells him. "I will see that she rests."

At this moment, a gentleman appears to beg a word with Horatio.

"Good Horatio, there are strangers arrived wishing to meet with thee."

Horatio frowns. "Strangers?" He and Anne exchange glances; he turns back to the gentleman. "I'll be with them straight." When the gentleman exits, Horatio turns a furrowed brow to Anne. "I cannot imagine who's come, nor what news they bring."

"Fortinbras?" I blurt, forgetting for a moment I am meant to be irrational. "Could it be word of his impending crusade to regain lands won of his father by our deceased King?"

Horatio bends me a queer look; I recover and slip back into my charade, turning to engage in conversation with the wall behind me.

"See to them," says Anne. "But I beg of thee, be safe."

"And thee," he whispers, touching her hair.

I watch Anne's gaze follow his departure, a violent ache surging up within me. Many times did I look after Hamlet in the same fashion. I envy her, even as I rejoice for her. And then, through a nearby window, comes a tremendous clamor.

I smile. "That would be Laertes. Right on time."

Anne and I are obliged to flatten ourselves against the wall as a messenger hurries in. "Know you the whereabouts of His Majesty?" he demands.

Anne points. "There, in yond chamber, with his Queen. What is the matter?"

(As if we did not know.)

"'Tis her brother." The messenger indicates me with a jerk of his head, then resumes his rush, shouting, "Save yourself, my lord!"

"Such theatrics!" I roll my eyes and sigh.

Anne giggles. Now Laertes, with his battalion, appears, and a noisier bunch of unwashed rabble I have never seen!

"Hello, Ophelia," he whispers.

"My dear brother," I reply, dipping my chin.

Now he roars: "Where is the King?"

I cover my ears, cast a glance at his band of rowdies. "Cavorting with the wrong crowd again, are we?" I tease.

"Not my usual fellows, sister. But well suited to this errand." He grins. "And they call me 'lord.'"

I giggle as he turns to address his partisans, ordering them to remain outside.

Some oppose the order, but Laertes insists. He pauses to snap me a wink, then draws his sword and bursts in upon Claudius. When the time is ripe, I shall intrude upon them to again make merry madness before the King. Laertes will play as though he is shocked to find me thus. Indeed, we do approach the climax of this fiction.

"I've one question," whispers Anne, as Laertes' followers withdraw. "While you are away from the castle, before I am to make my tragic announcement, your absence may be noticed. What am I to say, should anyone inquire after thee?"

"The truth," I suggest, bending her a shrewd smile.

"The truth?"

"Aye. Tell them I've gone for a swim."

## CHAPTER TWELVE

I KNEW NOT HOW DIVINE A PLAYER MY BROTHER could be. Sword swinging, he interrogates the King, shouting that he cares not about consequence. Gertrude is quite a wreck, but the evil King holds his calm; he does not shrink before the fury of his hunter, as he shriveled before me.

"Why, now," says Claudius, cloyingly, "you speak like a good child and a true gentleman. . . . I am guiltless of your father's death, and am most sensibly in grief for it."

At this, I sound a loud, wet raspberry!

The King hears me and motions to an attendant. "Let her come in."

"How now," stammers Laertes, "what noise is that?"

In answer, the attendant brings me forth, then steps away quickly, probably because I am picking at imaginary nits I pretend to spy in his hair. He leaves me in the center of the room, where I set to chewing my nails. My hair is more wild than before; I've tied wide sections into fat knots, which protrude from my scalp like furry growths. I begin to whistle.

"Oh heat, dry up my brains!" Laertes gasps. "Tears seven times salt, burn out the sense and virtue of mine eye!"

At the sound of his voice, I start, then wildly peruse the room. When at last I allow my eyes to meet his, I let out a squawk—part laugh, part choke—then genuflect as though methinks I see a saint. Laertes lets his sword fall to his side and gapes in disbelief. Tears grip his voice as he moves slowly toward me.

"Dear maid, kind sister, sweet Ophelia! Is't possible a young maid's wits should be as mortal as an old man's life?"

Once more I break into a song of death.

The Queen is crying. I wish not to dwell on that, and so I delve into the deep pockets of my skirts and withdraw . . . nothing! But to their eyes, it seems I've found a precious bundle. A bouquet, of course, which I hold as might a bride. I bury my face in the air where blooms, were there blooms, would be. I breathe deeply, then pluck an invisible offering from the bunch and hold my empty hand out to my brother.

"There's rosemary, that's for remembrance."

Slowly, dully, Laertes accepts the absence of rosemary from me.

"Pray you, love," I whisper loudly, "remember." I rise on tiptoe to kiss his chin, then laugh daintily, handing him another ghost. "And there is pansies, that's for thoughts."

His forlorn expression so amuses me that I must hurry off to keep from laughing. Gliding toward the King I go and wrinkle my nose at him. "There's fennel for you, and columbines."

He stares at me until I snatch his hand and slap the unseen flowers into it.

Now I sweep toward Gertrude and pretend to tuck a weedy ornament behind her ear. "There's rue for you, and here's some for me. We may call it herb of grace o' Sundays. You must wear your rue with a difference." Wrapping my arms around her neck, I whisper in her ear, "I would give you some violets, but they withered all when my father died." I pull back and smooth my skirts to add in a matter-of-fact tone, "They say he made a good end."

I lift my hands in a musical gesture as though asking them to join my song.

*"For bonny sweet Robin is all my joy."*

Laertes clutches his breast, howling. (Perhaps he does not like that the attention is all mine.) I sing, more loudly:

*"And will he not come again?*
*And will he not come again? No, no, he is dead,*

*Go to thy deathbed.*
*He never will come again."*

Waltzing gaily to the morbid words, I do not allow myself to think on them.

To think that he is gone. No triumph can restore him!

*"He is gone . . ."*

Hamlet.

He is gone. *". . . He is gone."*

My cover cracks, a cleft in the charade that invites true grief to creep beneath it. The words remind me. . . . *He never will come again.*

Bereavement breaks my strength, and I stumble. The Queen gasps; Laertes hastens to assist me, but I swipe at him, and he retreats.

I stand in the center of the hall. Alone.

There is no sound but for the ringing echo of my words, taunting me. He. Is. Gone.

*Gone.*

*Gone . . .*

Oh, I am cold. And yet my palms perspire. I struggle to recall the closing lines of the song. When I do, I manage only a whispered whimper; 'tis not part of this game, 'tis all I've the strength to utter:

*". . . God ha' mercy on his soul."*

A silence falls like autumn leaves around me. 'Tis as though I can reach out and catch pieces of it. Mayhap I shall stand here, shivering, forever.

But no. The song is done.

I give a graceless bow, then exit, calling weakly over my shoulder, "God be wi' you."

To my great relief, no one follows.

త త త

I find Anne in her room and tell her I am off to the brook.

"Wait one hour; at that time, you shall go to Gertrude, sobbing profusely, to tell her that you've found me drowned. Send someone to collect me—I will be lying sprawled on the bank, and very wet, at the first bend before the willow, where once I taught you to dive for coins."

Anne nods.

"Do not be overlong, as I do not wish to freeze to death."

"Someone will come for you in half an hour."

"Then you will meet me with Laertes."

She nods again.

"You do remember where, don't you?"

"Aye, Lia. I remember."

"Then say it, Anne. 'Tis crucial that we are clear on all points." I frown. "Where will you meet me?"

She mumbles a reply.

"Say it, Anne."

She draws a quivering breath. "One hour from now, as per our strategy, I will come for you, my friend . . . and find you in the morgue."

## CHAPTER THIRTEEN

No one thinks to dry a dead girl.

For this reason, I wait in my wet gown, shivering in a room I've only visited once before—'tis the morgue, far below stairs, beside the dungeon. Most fortunate 'tis that no one else has died of late. I've the place to myself.

The slab upon which I lie is cold and hard against my spine, the room is shadowy and dim, but my eyes have adjusted; I can make out a shelf which holds a collection of jars, no doubt containing the liquids and powders necessary to the practices and rites of burial. The alchemist in me longs to examine them.

At last there comes the rusty squeal of old hinges, then Anne's voice, whispering, "Lia! We have come!"

I sit up quickly on the slab, noting with an irreverent giggle that I am surely the only tenant of these chambers ever to have done so. "Here!" I announce.

They shuffle through the darkness. Finding me soaked, Laertes unfastens his jupon and removes it; I take it thankfully, slipping my arms into the sleeves.

"Ophelia," he cries, "I have most miraculous news!"

"I've spent an hour in this morbid cell," I inform him, "and have yet to see a single rat! No miracle may surpass that!"

"No? Would you feel thus were I to tell you that your Hamlet lives?"

His words reverberate in the darkness.

I shake my head, afraid even to half-believe. For half-belief is hope, and I have worn out what little hope I had.

Laertes takes my face in his hands. "He is alive, sister!"

"Alive?"

"Alive!"

Upon my soul, it is as though I can feel the stars halt their expeditions! The universe stills, awaits a word from me, but no word comes. Perhaps I have ceased to think, to breathe, to be.

Laertes shakes me. "Hear, Ophelia, let belief take hold. I have seen the proof. A letter, written in the Prince's character. England, it seems, has failed. Or else not tried. It matters not, except for this—your Hamlet lives! He comes! I cannot say for certain when, but he is bound for thee."

Oh, by the sweet breath of Saint Valentine, I am saved! Jubilant and prodigious truth! Suffering eludes me, now and forever, his life spared is mine regained. "Hamlet is alive!"

"Aye, sister!" Laertes hugs me. "And I would give the world to know your thoughts this moment!"

"This moment . . ." I begin, "this moment, I am thinking . . ."

"Yes?"

"Thinking that I shall need to wash my hair!"

At that, Anne lets out a snort of agreement.

"There is more to tell," Laertes says. "Even as he approaches, the King makes plans to kill him."

"Again?" I spring to my feet, throwing my arms wide in frustration. "Can that ass think of nothing other than murdering the Prince?"

"He has requested my assistance." Laertes smiles. "Which is a good thing."

I blink in amazement. "How so, pray tell?"

"The King hath schemed to arrange, upon the Prince's return, a game of swordplay between Hamlet and myself, citing the Prince's envy of my excellence at the sport as the bait to lure him to the match. Claudius will place a wager on the outcome, to increase the temptation."

"But such contests are conducted with blunted weaponry," I remind him. "How wouldst thou kill him with a bated blade?"

"Claudius depends upon the fact that Hamlet believes me a gentleman of honor, and will trust me to engage in sport according to the rules."

I frown a moment; then understanding dawns. "Hamlet will therefore neglect to inspect the foils, freeing you to choose a keen one. Or so imagines Claudius."

Laertes leans against the wall with a smug look. "Surely

the King will not quit his treachery till he sees with his own eyes Hamlet good and dead. It occurred to me that we could show him that very thing!"

My eyes brighten. "The poison!"

"Aye! I remembered the remarkable abilities you described of it, and the notion availed itself to me, even as Claudius did make his cruel proposal. I told him it would be unnecessary for me to run Hamlet through, for I'd purchased in my travels an unction so lethal that, should I anoint my rapier with it, I need only deliver Hamlet the scantest nick in order to take his life!"

"Did the King agree to it?"

"He did. But the fiend is cunning, and thought to support my plan with a contingency. On the chance I am unable to glance Hamlet with my blade, the King will have added the same poison to a chalice full with wine from which Hamlet will be invited to drink."

"'Tis perfect," I cry, clapping my hands. "Whether he be lanced or liquored, the aspect of death will come upon him just the same!" I turn to Anne. "And here is where Horatio may re-enter the campaign. After Hamlet's body has been deposited here, you will disclose all to Horatio, who shall then steal into this place and remove Hamlet to my father's cottage, where I will await him with the antidote."

"You forget," says Anne. "Hamlet's purpose remains to kill the King!"

"And he shall. For the King will think him dead, and

what better camouflage can there be than that? He can attack at will; the King will be defenseless. 'Tis a perfect strategy!"

But in some righteous place inside my heart, I know there is no perfection in murder.

Now my friend and brother take their leave.

I am alone, but for the echoes of a thousand final breaths drawn in this same darkness. Sinking to my knees, silent beside the slab, I offer a solemn prayer for the absolution of sins to be committed.

And I wait.

✿ ✿ ✿

One full day has passed since my drowning; this morning, a procession shall see me to my grave. Anne has come to ready me for my final journey; the coroner did argue heatedly at the outset, but Anne put forth such a fit of crying and pleading that at last he consented.

Round my neck hangs a heavy wooden cross, Hamlet's necklace and pendant hidden beneath. We have stowed a vial containing the antidote, which my father prepared using purpureum gathered from my mother's grave, inside the charm. The flask which holds the poison sits ready beside me on the slab. My father has surmised (though shakily at best) that the potion allows less than a quarter-day's sleep before giving over to pure death. Four hours only in which to conduct my fraudulent funeral, bear me off to his cottage near the croft, and administer the draft which shall—we most fervently hope—awaken life within me.

Anne has a second dose of the poison hidden in her reticule to be given to Laertes after the funeral. I wear a gown of lavender silk chosen by her. Presently, she is fussing with my hair.

"It need not be flawless, Anne." I sigh. "I am going to my grave, not to the altar to be wed!"

"Hush," she scolds. "I will not have it said that I sent thee to meet your maker with poorly done hair!"

I roll my eyes and endure the primping. "I do hope that in my falsified sleep I will retain the capacity to listen and comprehend. 'Twould be interesting to hear how I am mourned."

"Sick," snaps Anne, as she sets to arranging flowers in my hair. "I swear it, Lia, at times you are quite sick."

"Do you remember what you are to do when we reach the cemetery?"

"Aye. I am to make a most emotional scene, begging a moment alone with thee, before you are laid into the earth. I shall demand the others give me privacy to bid my friend farewell."

"Yes. And when they are gone . . ."

"Your father will carry you back to his cottage, to feed you the precious draft you carry in Hamlet's locket."

"Excellent." I squeeze her shoulder. "And you . . ."

She wrinkles her dainty nose. "I will remain beside your empty grave and use your father's spade to fill it up with dirt." She folds her arms. "Why must that grim task fall to me when it is *his* profession?"

"My father will need to be near me in the cottage," I remind her, "should anything with the antidote go awry."

"I do not relish the thought of filling in your grave," she grumbles.

"'Tis not as if I'll be in it!"

"Still . . ."

I interrupt her by opening the flask. It makes a small popping sound, then a hiss, as slim ribbons of silver smoke release themselves from within.

Anne bites her lip. "Strong stuff."

"Let us hope." I sniff the contents, then smile at her. "And now, a toast to my—what shall I call it?—impending near-death experience."

Anne shakes her head. "Thou art sick."

Raising the flask, I give Anne a most somber look. "To justice . . ." I grin. "I would 'justice' soon not die!"

"Witty."

"I thought so."

Without further discourse, I lift the flask to my lips. The flavor is nothing, mixed with air—not a taste but a sensation, rather like no sensation at all.

Oh, but 'tis a most potent nothing! Of a sudden, my eyelids grow impossibly heavy, my limbs leaden. A chill creeps upon my skin.

"Lia?"

"'Tis working!" I yawn, hugely. "I feel it. Oh, Anne, my heart—it beats; surely, but softly, softly, so softly. . . ."

"God save us!" Anne falls to her knees and makes the sign of the cross.

It is as though an invisible shroud's been wrapped around me. I recline with the weight of it, though it weighs less than light itself. The rhythm of my breath, though constant, is barely to be heard. I close my eyes. Sparks of darkness and a twinkling of twilight stars. I will my eyes to open, but they will not.

For one mad second I am gripped by panic! By the soul of Saint Vitus, on what fool's quest have I embarked, summoning death to my own device? What if my father's calculations prove faulty, and 'tis not four hours but four minutes before death?

I fear as I have never feared before, and the sleep enfolds me like fire.

But, soft . . .

Now comes a peace so perfect, so calm, and so complete, I can do no other than accept it. My hands, folded at my breast, cannot move, but I've no wish to move them. I feel the blood cooling in my veins.

Anne calls out to me. I hear her plainly but can make no answer. The poison perseveres, compressing me to a mere pinprick of awareness.

Stillness engulfs me; 'tis pure and plentiful. I am aware

of Anne near me, a vibration, a warmth, an energy. 'Tis like swimming in a dream.

From somewhere close comes knocking. Anne gasps and stammers, "Who's there?" The response is muffled. She opens the door. "What news?"

'Tis my father who responds. "He's been seen! The Prince."

Hamlet is near? And I—dead, mostly! Seeing me thus will surely break him! Even in this unholy slumber, I shudder. But there is no help for it, the plan must remain unaltered.

"How shall we proceed?" cries Anne.

"As planned," says my father. "There is no other."

"Mayhap you can intercept him to explain?"

No! My brain all but explodes with the wish to express itself. It is not yet time to apprise him of this plan. In truth, I fear he'd see fit to alter it, and that would be most disastrous. Hamlet must fence before the King! He must receive Laertes' thrust! So much hangs upon it!

"'Twould not be wise," my father replies. "Ophelia's scheme is sound; it does not allow for Hamlet knowing in advance, and so he shall not. His genuine grief at learning she is gone will only add reality to this drama." I sense a chuckle from him. "Perhaps I will revert to my old ways, draw upon my former profession, and do some playing of my own when he comes upon me at the grave."

"What mean you?" asks Anne, confused.

"Only that I shall entertain him a spell with silliness,

detain him as I play the clown. 'Tis the least I can do." He pauses to press a kiss to my cold forehead. "I am near to sobbing myself, seeing her so still."

"But her hair . . ." offers Anne. "'Tis lovely, is it not?"

My father laughs warmly, and then he is gone. Mere moments pass, and there comes a second knock.

Anne gasps, then whispers, "Lia . . . it is time!"

I feel Anne step aside to allow the pallbearers access. Now—motion, as they remove me from my stony berth and bear me away.

Mayhap there is sunshine. Difficult to tell, I sense only the sway of shadow and light across my eyelids. Music, a hymn, a tempo most macabre.

The procession has begun.

## CHAPTER FOURTEEN

'TIS NEAR A MILE FROM THE OUTER CURTAIN OF the castle to the hallowed ground.

The mourners come behind me: I imagine Laertes first, beside the doctor of divinity, then Claudius and Gertrude, Anne, Horatio, and all the rest—courtiers, retainers, and servants who knew me while I lived. (Barnardo has most likely not come. Mayhap he fears my spirit will haunt him; were I a spirit, I would indeed.)

The pallbearers halt now, and the clergyman from his book recites a line or two on my behalf toward heaven. His speech is markedly shorter than those I remember from burials which I've attended. I hear the papery thud of the closing book, followed by Laertes' voice, demanding a lengthier ceremony.

The cleric gives a windy sigh and explains to my brother

that he has said all he can, indeed, more, my death being "doubtful."

Doubtful? As in suspect? Hell's eyes, this is news to me! Think they that I died at my own hand? That was not the illusion I wished to create. How dare they e'en suggest that I would indulge in such a cowardly act! Me, Ophelia—so weak as to willingly abandon life? 'Tis unjust and wrong I be remembered thus. I *drowned*! 'Twas the river's doing, the work of the undertow (at least, 'tis how it was meant to appear)! A fie on't!

Someone kneels beside me. Even with my diminished breath I recognize the leathery-clean scent of my brother. "Lay her i' th' earth, and from her fair and unpolluted flesh may violets spring!"

Well, now, that is quite lyrical. When I awaken, I will remember to thank him for his tribute.

The Queen approaches; her heavy gown rustles, and there is a clanking of bracelets as she scatters petals o'er me. "Sweets to the sweet, farewell. I hoped thou shouldst have been my Hamlet's wife; I thought thy bride-bed to have decked, sweet maid, and not have strewed thy grave."

Good it is that I am unable to form tears, or surely I would cry at so heartfelt an avowal.

Then Laertes shouts in a quavering voice, "Hold off the earth awhile"—next I know, my lifeless body is pulled against his strong chest—"till I have caught her once more in my arms."

Suddenly there comes the sound of hard footsteps advancing in the dirt, another voice, tight with unshed tears, deafening with despair. "What is he whose grief bears such an emphasis?"

Hamlet! Here! At my funeral. Cursed timing! 'Tis not good, not good at all.

I am aware of scuffling around me, a grunt, a growl, the hollow thump of a punch well landed. Could it be? Heaven save me, it is! These *boys* are fighting! At my *funeral!*

The truth of it dawns on me harshly. Laertes is acting, aye, but Hamlet—he does not know that this be staged! His grief, his heartache, his anger—all genuine! God help him.

There are shouts from the procession as the King orders them separated.

A sliver of one second and Hamlet is there beside me, his hands gentle in my hair, a tear spilling from his eye to drop upon my lips; I can taste the salt of it.

From the bottom of his soul he brings forth a roar. "I loved Ophelia!"

My name thunders circles upon itself as his bold and unabashed declaration rolls o'er the hillside. I am undone by his suffering.

"Forty thousand brothers could not, with all their quantity of love, make up my sum."

*And twice that do I love thee, sweet Prince!* I say in silence.

A moment more does Hamlet bait Laertes, then, surrendering to his sadness, makes a thrashing exit. The King directs Horatio to follow him.

I am aware of Claudius murmuring something to my brother and then of Anne feigning hysteria as she throws herself upon my corpse, demanding a space of absolute solitude to bid me a good-bye. The mourners do not argue.

Before leaving, Laertes bestows a kiss, which becomes a whisper.

"'Twill never be said your funeral was dull, sister. I pray you not be angry, and bid you remember one important fact. . . ." He pauses, chuckling. "'Twas Hamlet who started it."

## CHAPTER FIFTEEN

WITH GREAT CARE DOES MY FATHER BEAR ME HOME.

I am laid upon a feathery pallet, anxious to regain use of myself. Hands, eyes, legs, lips . . . longing to rebel against this imposed placidity.

My father removes the crucifix, revealing Hamlet's pendant beneath. Deftly, he unlocks the charm and withdraws the vial.

"Patience, daughter," he says gently. "The potion need be well shaken. Shall I tell thee of my meeting with your Prince? 'Twas great sport! I recalled you told me he had a fondness for wordplay, so I was most selective in my phrasing. I roused from the poor fellow several good belly laughs before he took in the heart-wrenching sight of your funeral. I played the dunce, a smiling simpleton shoveling skulls at him—in a nice way, of course—and he was most ponderous of them. One formerly belonging to a man called

Yorick especially caught his attention. Wise is Prince Hamlet, and thoughtful, to be sure, but I must say, the lad can carry himself off now, can't he? Once he gets talking!"

Gently, he lifts my head and feeds me the elixir.

It is nothing like the one that came before it. This one carries the flavor of fire! 'Tis as if I've brought lightning to my lips! A liquid blaze, searing my tongue.

"Swallow," my father commands. "It burns, I know, but you must!"

There is a tingling in my fingertips now, a strong prickling through my legs and arms. I would writhe if I could.

Panic spikes in my father's voice. "Ophelia?"

I fear the antidote fails me! Might true death from false death derive?

There begins a warming in my blood, which suddenly goes hot. And the prickling of pins turns at once to knives, stabbing. I make to cry out in pain, but my voice has been burned off.

My hands tremble but will not move.

A swirling blackness swells behind my eyes. I fight to force through it, but it rages like a tempest. It bursts forth from me, swallows me, surrounds me like smoke. I spiral skyward, propelled by flames. Mayhap I have misjudged the safe boundaries of the antidote and slept too long; or perhaps this potion was poison greater than that which it was meant to undo.

*Wake! I pray . . . wake!*

"Daughter!" My father's tone is taut with alarm. He shakes me; it only causes the stabbing to grow worse. "Ophelia!"

The fire blazes; the prickling increases until 'tis no feeling at all. Less than none, only the memory of feeling. O God! Surely I am closer to dying than living. In silence, I demand my life return but fear that it escapes me in the smoke of the black storm.

I hear my father leaving. Fleet footsteps, the door . . . then hours, days, a lifetime. God's blood, does he abandon me to this merciless passing?

No! He is back, beside me, with water from the brook, of which he administers a great cool quantity.

"Drink!" my father orders.

'Tis not choice but instinct allows the liquid in. I am still too dead to swallow, but I feel it streaming down the charred passage of my throat, diluting the devilish draft that burns me.

"More," he commands, tilting the cup again. This time, I manage small gulps; the water sputters from my lips, dribbles down my chin.

And slowly . . . the blackness lifts.

Slowly, spinning away as I push through it. And now the fire subsides. My blood is once again temperate in my veins, coursing through me, willing me to wake. A breath; another, as I note the quickening of my pulse, the pure and patient pattern of my heart. I open my eyes.

My father hovers over me, white with fear, and whispers, "Child."

In a voice like clouds I whisper, "Strong stuff."

He holds me close, crying, laughing. "Methinks 'twas too much of a good thing."

"Aye, but it performs, and that is what counts." I pick up the vial; the thick dregs of the antidote cling to the inside. "It wants a small correction, which I will note in Mother's journal, in large, bold characters."

"What instruction wilt thou include?"

Tapping the vial with my finger, I answer, "Just add water."

ॐ ॐ ॐ

My father's apprentice is smitten with Anne. His name is Tuck; he is young—perhaps twelve—and gangly. He has loved her from the moment he came upon her shoveling dirt into my idle grave.

Anne returned from her task with her linen dress dusty, her face enchantingly smudged, and Tuck trailing after her. At supper, the boy rests his chin upon his fist and stares at her.

It has been hours since my awakening. Father has prepared a stew of venison, turnips, and onions, on which we four dine in the candlelight.

Anne, who does much of the cooking at Elsinore, compliments my father on the meal. "The secret is in the seasoning," he says.

Recipes?! Am I to listen to talk of ginger and raisins when I can barely sit still, knowing Hamlet is so close, and mourning me at that? "I must see him!" I shout; 'tis at least the tenth time.

And also for the tenth time, my father reminds me that I can hardly stroll into the castle alive after the entire population of it has just seen me buried.

"He is correct," says Anne.

At the sound of her voice, Tuck jumps, toppling his cup of cider, which spills into his lap. He springs from his seat, knocking Anne's cup in the bargain and soaking his sleeve.

My father sighs. "Hang the clothes near the fire, Tuck. They will be dry by morning. Meantime, you'll find my spare breeches on a peg behind the door."

Anne and I excuse ourselves and wait out of doors while Tuck changes clothes.

Indeed, I am thinking, Tuck's pants will be dry by morning. And by morning, I'll be gone.

ॐ ॐ ॐ

Tuck's tattered garb is a good fit. Anne says the way the breeches hug the curve of my hips is scandalous.

"Scandalous, aye, but comfortable! No wonder men keep them for themselves."

In truth, I can recall no other feeling so liberating as this! I may run, jump, kick high as an unbroken stallion. I would ne'er have believed such power could come of wearing pants!

"'Tis yet another injustice against our sex." I sigh.

Anne shrugs. "If they are that wondrous, perhaps one day women shall be permitted to don them."

"'Twill never happen!" I assure her. "The male of the species could not abide such a threat to his authority. A female in braies? No man would allow it."

"Mayhap not." Anne smirks, her eyes twinkling. "But should one ever happen to catch a glimpse of thy backside in a pair of them, he might be persuaded to change his mind."

We have just reached the outer wall of the bailey. The east unfurls ribbons of golden daylight. Elsinore is quiet.

I've taken an old hood of my father's, which I now place o'er my hair, tucking the long waves up beneath it. Tuck's jupon blouses sufficiently in front to obscure any sign of my femininity.

"I shall enter through the kitchen," I tell Anne. "No doubt you were missed last night, but I think 'twould be best you remain out of sight until the fencing contest. It would not do for you to be questioned."

She nods. "There is a toolshed beyond the kitchen garden. The old hayward keeps a Bible there; I shall be pleased to spend this day secluded, reading scripture."

"Excellent. For my part, I will find an inconspicuous spot to await the fencing contest, though I would much prefer making directly to Hamlet's chamber, to throw myself into his arms."

"Better not to." Anne giggles. "Such an act would surely frighten him to death!"

I smile. "You mean because he would think 'twas the embrace of a ghost."

"No, I mean because he would think 'twas the embrace of a boy!"

"Ah," I say, waggling my eyebrows. "I've no fear of that. For, while I am confident my costume will fool the majority of this castle, I know one thing for certain."

"And that is . . . ?"

I pat my bottom, wiggle it inside the braies. "That Hamlet would recognize my backside anywhere!"

At that, Anne gasps. "See?" she mutters. "Sick."

## CHAPTER SIXTEEN

IT HAS BEEN A MOST HUMILIATING DAY. IN MY BOY'S attire I've stirred no suspicion as to my true identity; however, the costume has placed me in a rather outrageous position.

A chambermaid has taken a shine to me! I believe her name to be Sigrid. She is plump and blonde and pretty, but, God's truth, a more brazen girl hath never been!

She caught sight of me loitering in the arcade, and apparently set her cap for the lad she thought I was. I have been forced to spend the better part of the morning ducking round corners to avoid her. And I have been skillful at it. Until now.

"There thou art!"

"O God . . ." Quickly, I remember what I am about and deepen my voice. "Have I not told you . . ."

"Yes, yes, you have told me. Thou art spoken for. But you've yet to tell me your lover's name."

I nearly blurt out *Hamlet.*

Giggling, Sigrid approaches me as a hungry lioness might approach a wounded gazelle; I am cornered. "Calm thyself, boy. 'Tis not anything permanent I be wanting."

"Say you?"

"You may scurry back to your peasant love, once I've had what I am after."

"And that would be . . . ?"

"Only a tumble with such a bonny lad as thee."

A *tumble?* My mouth drops open in shock and disgust. Hell's blood, first Barnardo, now this! I am not safe in this castle no matter what my gender!

"You cannot make me," I sputter in my low voice.

"Watch me."

'Tis true, the trollop has me by at least twenty pounds. Even if I were a boy, 'twould be difficult for me to overtake her. She advances again, her chubby chin raised in pursuit of my lips.

It is now that the guards Marcellus and Barnardo happen by. The sight of Barnardo makes my heart slam inside my chest: for if he discovers me I am lost for certain.

"What, ho!" cries Marcellus. "Sigrid! Be thou at it again?"

Barnardo frowns, struggling to make sense of the scene. Once he does, he laughs.

"He's but a mere slip of a boy!" Marcellus says. "Why, your charms will spoil him for sure."

"If he lives through it," Barnardo adds.

Sigrid turns and winks at him. "You did."

(I am close to retching at the thought of that.)

"Leave the lad alone," Marcellus scolds. "Look at him. His teeth chatter at the very idea of a romp with you."

Sigrid gives me a long, considering look, then shrugs and turns away as though I'd evaporated into thin air. She smiles at the guards. "Well, then, what of *your* teeth, Barnardo?"

"Come this way, wench, and I will show you!"

When they have gone, I breathe deeply, relieved. Marcellus watches them go, then turns a kind look to me.

"Are you all right, lad?" he asks, grinning. "Siggy did not harm thee?"

"No, sir."

"Shook you up, though."

"Aye, a little." His manner is so friendly that I accidentally smile at him.

His eyes round first, then narrow. "Do . . . do I know thee, boy?"

I lower my face abruptly. "No, sir."

"Hmm. For a moment . . ." He shakes his head, then chuckles. "Ah, well . . . just remember that you are now beholden to Barnardo, for 'twas his ready appetite that saved thee!" At his own jest he laughs ringingly.

I turn to go, and mutter, "Good day, sir."

Marcellus claps me on the back; it nearly sends me flying. "God keep you, lad. If you hurry, you may catch what action remains of the fencing contest."

"Fencing?" My head snaps upward again. "Then it has begun?"

"'Twas from whence we came, Barnardo and I. At the time of our departure, Prince Hamlet held a small advantage, having delivered Laertes one hit. . . . Lad?"

I am already halfway down the long corridor which leads to the great hall.

᭖ ᭖ ᭖

Anne awaits me at the entrance. She reports that there are enough spectators in the hall so that we may hide easily among them, but something in her tone troubles me.

"What is wrong, Anne?"

"Oh, Lia! Indulge me a moment that I may tell my horrid news of Horatio!"

"Horrid news?" I peer through a gap in the crowd, and frown. "It cannot be anything too awful, Anne. He is standing right over there in Hamlet's camp, and looks the picture of health."

"Mayhap, but inside he is aching! 'Twas all told to me by one of the pages when I emerged from the shed not half an hour ago. Horatio had posted him on lookout for me in the garden."

"Lookout?"

"Horatio had every servant in residence on alert! He believes me gone."

"Gone?"

"Aye. No one has seen me since your funeral, and Horatio fears the worst. By the page's account, he rode out last night to search for me and did not return till noon today, exhausted and distressed. He immediately dispatched several foot soldiers to continue the quest and spent the hours that followed on his knees in the chapel."

"I do not understand the problem, Anne. Why do you not simply go to him and demonstrate your presence?"

"At the moment, he is otherwise involved."

She is right, of course. Loyal Horatio supports Hamlet in this contest. A more careful look at him tells me that Anne does not exaggerate; clearly, he is miserable.

"As soon as this ends—with Hamlet poisoned and left for dead—you can explain all to Horatio. Unfortunately, friend, we can do nothing now but wait this out."

Anne sighs, nods. I take her hand. We make our way into the hall to find a place amid the onlookers.

"How goes it?" I ask a nobleman standing near.

"A fair amount of perspiration," he says, laughing. "And grunting."

I roll my eyes. "What else?"

"The King hath offered Hamlet the prize of a pearl."

I watch as Claudius drinks from a chalice, then drops the pearl into it. "No doubt the pearl carries the poison," I whisper to Anne.

Claudius extends the cup to Hamlet. "Here's to thy health," he booms.

Although I know that he is to be poisoned ultimately, and, furthermore, that I carry in my pocket the means to reverse it, I cannot help but sigh with relief when my love declines the cup.

"I'll play this bout first," he tells Claudius.

Laertes' eyes dart from the cup to his own weapon; mayhap he is thinking the same as I.

Frowning slightly, the King returns the cup to the small table that stands between his throne and Gertrude's.

"Come!" Hamlet dares.

Again, the swords whistle, slicing the very air to ribbons. Hamlet thrusts to earn a second point.

"Another hit!" he boasts, nodding to his opponent. "What say you?"

"A touch, a touch," Laertes admits. "I do confess."

The suspense brings an itch to my fingertips, and I find myself bouncing from one boot to the other. I know how 'twill end—with Hamlet scraped and sleeping—but, still, 'tis sheer excitement to observe. They are expert, graceful, determined. For all their preposterous ways, boys are glorious to watch at sport.

And now the Queen calls out to Hamlet. "Here, Hamlet, take my napkin; rub thy brows."

Her doting causes a ripple of laughter through the assembly. The nobleman beside me shakes his head and elbows me hard; of a sudden, I find myself shoved to the front of the crowd, just as Hamlet approaches his mother. His path will bring him mere inches from where I stand. Quickly, I bow my head and keep it down.

I do not see what the Queen does next; it is only because Claudius speaks that I realize what she is about.

"The Queen carouses to thy fortune, Hamlet!" she calls.

"Good madam," replies Hamlet, but o'er his words comes Claudius's troubled voice:

"Gertrude, do not drink."

"I will, my lord," she replies blithely. "I pray you, pardon me."

I snap my head up, but before the scream can form itself, she has already swallowed a fine mouthful! I whip around to regard Claudius. He is looking suddenly quite pale, and well he should, for he does not know the full of it. Indeed, he believes the poison fatal! And the beast did not attempt to snatch away the cup!

The Queen places the cup on the table; her lips glisten from the wine.

Anne recognizes the problem immediately. "Exactly how much of that antidote didst thou brew?" she asks.

"Enough," I answer.

As Hamlet allows his mother to wipe his face, I notice that Laertes is engaged in a whispered conversation with the King. I hope he is suggesting they move swiftly with their dark scheme; time, as he knows, is against us.

"Come for the third, Laertes!" taunts Hamlet. "You do but dally!"

Grinning, Laertes returns his barbs; for a moment, I am reminded of the way they played together as children. 'Tis almost easy to forget the corruption that surrounds us now. I force myself to look at Gertrude. Her skin has turned a sickly gray; I see her eyes flutter, then close.

Eager to be done, Laertes charges the Prince; a flick of the blade tears Hamlet's sleeve as the tainted point of the weapon presses into his shoulder. The room falls silent.

Laertes does not move, watching the emotion sweep o'er the Prince's face, flash in his eyes. Mayhap Hamlet doubts his own senses; indeed, he did not expect such pain from a blunted sword. But a glance tells him he bleeds. His bellow breaks the stillness.

And now a tussle; the Prince deftly forces an exchange of swords. 'Tis brilliant, aye, but most contrary to our plan. Hamlet wields the sharp one now! Laertes dodges him, jerking sideways, but Hamlet is nimble, and with a shout delivers a long, jagged gash to Laertes' chest.

"Part them!" cries the King.

"Nay, come again!" shouts Hamlet.

Across the platform, Gertrude attempts to rise from her throne. But the poison is swift, and she has not the strength to balance herself. She sways, then drops to the floor.

Several servants fly to her aid. Claudius seems paralyzed upon his throne.

Horatio, still engrossed in the match, sweeps his gaze from Hamlet to Laertes. "They bleed on both sides!" he announces, then turns to the Prince. "How is it, my lord?"

Hamlet does not answer. Already, I recognize the poison's

aspect. The color drains from him, and his eyes drop though he struggles to keep them open. The same is true of my brother.

Laertes turns a sleepy but loathing glare to the King. His legs betray him now and give way; he drops to his knees dramatically. "I am justly killed with mine own treachery."

Anne bends a look at me. "He overacts."

I nod.

Hamlet is trying to reach the Queen but is stayed by those who would tend to his wound.

"How does the Queen?" he demands.

Claudius blanches. "She swoons to see them bleed," he bluffs in a hollow voice.

But the Queen is wise to it now. "No, no, the drink, the drink!" She spreads her shivering arms, a last embrace for no one. "Oh, my dear Hamlet! The drink, the drink! I am poisoned."

I do not know why I tremble, for I have orchestrated all of this. But I have seen one mother die, and though this death is temporary, 'tis still most painful. It is as though, in her closing moments, all her virtue is restored. In the final flutter of her eyes, I see her deep regret, her sorrow, her need to be forgiven. She is the Gertrude I once cherished. Oh, 'tis gut-wrenching to witness the waning of such grace, such goodness, e'en as I know this death is finite.

Hamlet is wild now, even as the exhaustion stalks him. "Oh, villainy! Treachery! Seek it out."

But he need not seek it, for it comes to him in Laertes' confession. "It is here, Hamlet," he coughs, pointing to the Prince's rapier to indicate its tainted tip. "Hamlet, thou art slain." From his knees, at the center of the platform, he pants, fighting to remain alert. "No med'cine in the world can do thee good," he lies.

'Tis of course for Claudius's benefit he saith such. Hamlet stares at him, weakening rapidly, battling to grasp my brother's meaning.

"The treacherous instrument is in thy hand, unbated and envenomed. . . . The King, the King's to blame."

"The point envenomed too!" Hamlet reels, dragging the hand that does not hold his weapon down the pallor of his face. He staggers toward the King. "Then, venom, do thy work."

He slashes the blade through the air, catching Claudius near his ribs.

The King grunts, doubles over. Some in the crowd call "Treason!" as the King begs for help.

Now Hamlet stumbles to the table to snatch the cup. Taking hold of Claudius, he presses it to his lips and forces the wine down his gullet.

"Here, thou incestuous, murd'rous, damned Dane!" he shouts with what little strength remains within him. "Drink this potion."

The King chokes, gags, ingesting the ruined wine.

Eyes flashing, Hamlet releases the King. "Follow my mother."

I watch, heart thudding, as the pearl which bore the poison drops from the cup and rolls 'cross the platform, where Laertes scoops it up.

"He is justly served," says my brother, on a cough. "It is a poison tempered by himself." Holding the pearl between his fingers, Laertes gives the Prince a beseeching look. "Exchange forgiveness with me, noble Hamlet. Mine and my father's death come not upon thee, nor thine on me."

I glance around to check how the crowd receives it. A tear meanders down the cheek of the nobleman beside me. Brilliant Laertes. He has provided all with an ending most acceptable.

In a withering but honest voice, Hamlet accepts and grants the absolution. His chin falls to his chest, he lurches forward. Good Horatio is at his elbow to hold him up.

"I am dead, Horatio." 'Tis spoken as though he can't quite believe it. He falls against his friend. Anne gasps. I wonder when I began to weep.

"Horatio, I am dead." His head drops to Horatio's shoulder. "Thou livest; report me and my cause aright to the unsatisfied."

But Horatio too is weeping. To my astonishment he takes the near-empty goblet and makes to drink from it.

Again, Anne gasps. "He would take his life!"

"He believes you dead," I whisper, "and his closest friend does die in his embrace. He is racked with despair."

But before Horatio can bring the goblet to his lips, Hamlet summons the might to grab it.

"Let go!" is the Prince's husky demand; the cup clatters to the floor. With eyes distant and desperate, he begs his friend remain alive to tell his story.

From a distance comes the sound of drums; without warning, a shot rings out.

Hamlet surrenders to the poison now, and would fall to the floor were it not for Horatio's firm hold.

Many of the assembly rush to the window; from there the report is hollered back to us.

"They descend upon us—Norway and England at once!"

"Fortinbras comes to conquer Denmark," cries the nobleman beside me, "and on his way salutes with shots those who arrive from English shores."

"Why come the English?" asks Anne.

I know not; my eyes are fixed on Hamlet as he nears his transient slumber. Horatio leans closer, for the Prince's voice has become a mere wisp of sound.

"I cannot hear," says Anne from behind me. "What says the Prince?"

"Fortinbras will become the new lord of Elsinore, and Hamlet is for it," I tell her. "He charges Horatio to impart all of what hath occurred to this new King, so that he may set it right."

Hamlet heaves a heavy breath. He does not see me rush forth to be by his side, for his eyes close now in earnest. I press close to him, wanting to comfort him, to assure him that his spirit does not dissolve within him.

But to him this death is true death, and he slips from the world with one final, perfect thought.

Saith Hamlet, "The rest is silence."

*Silence.*

Carefully, Horatio lowers his friend to the floor.

All present bow their heads in prayer as Horatio continues. "Good night, sweet Prince, and flights of angels sing thee to thy rest."

I reach down to touch Hamlet's cheek. 'Tis now that Horatio notices me. He looks blank for a moment. His brow wrinkles as he tries to place me, this grubby boy who weeps for the Prince. His face takes on a stunned expression. He drags me away from Hamlet to inquire: "Ophelia?" He blinks, mouth open. "But . . ."

I press a finger to my lips to hush him. Before I can speak, however, more drum noise assaults us, this time from within.

Horatio is alert now. I scramble back into the crowd. Next I know, the hall is filled with flags and attendants, and behind them strolls Fortinbras of Norway. Three men join them, whom I surmise to be the ambassadors from England. I do not tarry to hear what follows. There is something I must do.

I open the door to my chamber and step inside. A choke of sadness escapes my throat, for I know with all certainty that I will ne'er again enter this place. 'Twas here my mother rocked me as an infant in her arms; 'twas here she returned to me, a smoky vision with most miraculous news. 'Twas here that Hamlet and I . . .

I shall not dwell on't. I press the tears from my eyes and hurry to gather what I came for.

When I leave, I close the door behind me.

Hope awaits. I don't look back.

I return to the hall to find Fortinbras alone, surveying his new realm with a serious expression. All the "dead" have been removed, with the exception of Claudius. I expect servants will come for him anon. At this moment, I know, Horatio and Anne are having Laertes and Hamlet brought from the morgue to my father's cottage. I smile, recalling the shocked look in Horatio's eyes at finding me alive. 'Twas nothing compared with the joy he must feel at seeing Anne.

Now I step o'er Claudius's body and boldly approach young Fortinbras.

He eyes me strangely. He is uncommonly large; even his voice is gigantic. "I did not expect the men of Denmark would be so delicate."

At first, I do not catch the reference, and cock an eyebrow at him somewhat rudely. "Hm? Oh!" 'Tis now I remember how I am dressed. Swallowing hard, I remove my hood, letting my long hair cascade around my shoulders.

"I am not a man, my lord. I am Ophelia, a lady of this court."

Now I have his attention.

"A lady of this court in tattered breeches?" Fortinbras folds his arms across his chest and smiles slightly.

I ignore the warm invitation in his voice. "Permit me, Your Majesty, but I would tell thee of the turn of events that brings us to this peculiar situation."

He looks at me in Tuck's braies. "I find myself very willing to listen to anything you might have to say. Pray, give me your story."

I draw a deep breath. "Well . . . it began with the King that's dead. His brother, who lies here, appearing quite dead himself, poisoned him. 'Twould have gone unknown, his death being thought natural, except that the ghost told the Prince."

"Ghost?"

"Of the deceased King Hamlet. He came upon the guard's watch and told of his murder to the Prince. But not before his evil brother had married his wife."

"The Queen? She who has just been carried away to the morgue?"

"Aye. They married hastily, and Claudius became King. It was then that the ghost appeared to reveal the truth. The Prince was reluctant to believe the word of a ghost, of course, and so he set out to prove that his uncle, now his stepfather, was to blame, in order that he might rightfully avenge his father's death. 'Twas then the Prince went mad."

Fortinbras lowers his brows. "The Prince went mad."

"Aye, but not really. 'Twas feigned, you see, for the purpose of drawing out the King."

"The King that's dead?"

"No, the forged one, his uncle." I motion with my head to the body behind me. "That one, who merely looks dead. Hamlet pretended madness, which the general populace of this castle did attribute to my refusal to return his love. He also reconstructed the argument of a play. A play performed by traveling players, amended by the Prince to describe the murderous deed committed by Claudius against his brother. Claudius was most upset by it, leading the Prince, and, for that matter, myself, to accept the accusation put forth by the ghost. Alas, our plan went slightly awry here; Hamlet accidentally killed my father. . . ."

Fortinbras gives me an incredulous look.

"Well, not my father; but the man believed by all to be my father." I pause to smile. "That, my lord, is another story altogether."

"Hmm."

"Claudius then sent Hamlet to England, requesting he be put to death. Anne found that out."

"Anne?" Before I can begin my explanation regarding Anne, he holds up his hands and says in a resigned voice, "Anne. Yes. Go on."

"I was most despondent, as you might guess, to imagine Hamlet dead, and more determined to prove the King guilty. 'Twas then that I put on my own antic disposition, and, if I do say, 'twas quite convincing. About this time, the King commenced to make lewd advances toward me, and as I would rather be dead than touched by him, I died. Not wholly, merely long enough to be thought buried. 'Twas accomplished with the use of a poison which gives the illusion of death. 'Twas quite useful, too, for 'tis that same poison that is responsible for the seeming death of Prince Hamlet, my brother, the Queen"—I jerk my thumb in the direction of Claudius's cadaverous form—"and him."

Fortinbras stares at me a long moment.

"Am I to understand," he says at last, "that the King is still alive?"

"Aye. And it falls to you to decide if he shall remain thus. Claudius looks dead, but 'tis only sleep which has besieged him." I reach into the pocket of my breeches and produce a vial containing the antidote. "This will save him, should you deem him deserving of salvation. You are lord of Elsinore now, so 'tis up to you to choose."

Fortinbras studies the King and frowns. "I have much to arrange here," he mutters thoughtfully. "I would see the castle, then the grounds. And 'twould be good to view my chambers, mayhap bathe as well." He shrugs, then turns to me. "I shall decide all of this on the morrow, then, for I find that I am hungry, and should much enjoy dining with a lady fair as thee."

Dinner? At a time such as this? Does he jest? I blink at him in disbelief.

"Well, Ophelia? Surely this business will wait till—"

"No!" I thunder in reply. "That is, no thank you, Highness."

He stares at me, his eyes solemn. 'Tis as though I can see the weight of his duty bearing down upon him. He sighs gustily.

"No dinner, then. A pity." For a moment, his eyes brighten with mischief. "Unless you would join me for the purpose of providing more thorough edification regarding this slumberous villain's crimes."

I reach beneath my tunic and withdraw the scroll on which I inscribed the extent of Claudius's crimes. "'Tis all written here. I would ask thee to strongly consider his offenses in naming his fate."

He takes the scroll. "And the Queen? Does she merely sleep as well?"

I nod.

"What dost thou recommend with regard to her judgment? Would you have me spare her life?"

"I would, my lord. There is much that is good in her. I beseech thee, revive her, and give her a place in this court. The poison becomes lethal in the fifth hour; therefore, I ask that you see to Her Majesty's cure quickly."

"As you desire, Lady Ophelia." Fortinbras of Norway takes the vial, and my hand as well, which he draws slowly to his lips. "'Tis becoming clear to me that, even did I wish it, I could deny you nothing."

Men! 'Tis an act of immeasurable will to refrain from rolling my eyes.

"I have one additional request, my liege, if I may."

"You need only speak it."

"In a chamber above the stairs, the one which o'erlooks the bailey to the east, you will find a rather impressive collection of wildflowers and herbs. I would ask that you see to it they are tended. It is my opinion that Sigrid, the chambermaid, is in dire need of a more productive pastime than the one with which she presently occupies herself. And so I suggest it be Sigrid to whom my flowers are entrusted. Beyond the stream, at the end of the cemetery path, she will find the gravedigger's cottage. He will instruct her in the care and employment of these precious plants."

Fortinbras nods slowly, taking it all in. "So . . . the truth of it, then, is that the Lady Ophelia—who, despite her lovely hair and pretty eyes, wears old boots and boy's breeches—has managed to create a most miraculous potion, which she employed to stage her own death, thereby successfully indicting a murderer, which is to say defeat a King, yet in the end her primary concern is for the health and well-being . . . of her flowers?"

"You are correct, sir."

He turns my hand over in his and presses a soft kiss against my palm. "You are remarkable, you know. Must you leave Elsinore, Ophelia?"

"I must." *And soon!*

"So be it." Reluctantly, he releases my hand. "But know you this, dear one. The loss of thee is a blow from which I will not soon recover."

"You are young, sire. You shall get over it."

He laughs out loud. The sound is warm and sincere. At once, I understand that he is a good man. For the first time in many months, I feel there may be hope for this place.

"Godspeed, Lady Ophelia."

Ignoring my boy's costume, I offer him my most elegant curtsy. And I am off.

# CHAPTER SEVENTEEN

MY FATHER TENDS TO LAERTES; HORATIO ASSISTS me with Hamlet. Anne has already wrapped his wound, having given it a thorough cleansing whilst I readied the attenuated antidote. She did the same for Laertes, whose injury was slightly more severe.

The mood in the cottage is both hopeful and solemn. No one speaks; we seem to know by some good magic what is required of each of us. Indeed, I have not uttered so much as a sound since returning here from Elsinore.

Now Horatio holds the Prince up by his shoulders so that he is almost sitting. I use one trembling finger to part his lips, then gently pour the watery mixture in.

Wiping my palms on the front of my breeches, I notice how my knees quiver within them. In my heart, I pray fiercely that my father has rightly surmised the necessary proportion of water to repair the antidote and spare Hamlet and Laertes the nightmare I endured. But 'tis nigh the close of that mysterious fourth hour; they have slept far longer than I. What, then, if their extended sleep requires the potion at its strongest? My thoughts churn, and I cannot stop the trembling of my hands.

Anne and Horatio stand above the Prince, staring hopefully down at him. In truth, I cannot bear to watch. The bluish tint to his lips terrifies me, and the blood-soaked bandage is none too pleasant a sight either. Since I refuse to swoon for any reason, I turn my back to Hamlet.

This is not cowardice; this is worry. And I am not at all ashamed of that.

Across the room, Laertes, who drank first, begins to stir. My heart leaps, and my soul shouts for joy, but still I make no sound, no move other than to lean forward and press my palms against the table. Were I not to, I fear I would crumble in an anxious heap.

Laertes has opened his eyes to find himself in a stranger's arms. In the next instant, though, he understands.

"My noble sire."

Our father smiles, does not try to hide his tears.

Laertes' voice is hushed and happy as he studies the image so like his own. "I see that it is you I may thank for these tousled waves through which so many French ladies did delight in running their fingers."

(I cannot help but roll my eyes at that!)

Would that I could cross the room to welcome my brother back, but I am too reliant upon this tabletop. I watch as the color returns to his face, the brilliance to his eyes, which are so like those of the man who holds him. 'Tis lucky I need not introduce them: in my current state, I would find it difficult to form the words.

Behind me, Anne and Horatio whisper nervously, for still no move does Hamlet make.

*Flights of angels, change thy course. Sing him* here, *to me!*

When Laertes groans in pain, Anne fetches fresh water from the fire and goes to him. She removes the blood-stained bandage, and again sets to rinsing the deep gash in Laertes' chest; he winces as Anne applies a salve. I am so lost in watching her tend him that I almost do not hear . . .

"Ophelia?"

I remain where I am, bent over the table, not turning, for I fear I've only dreamed the sound: even if Hamlet has revived, he would find no reason to speak my name; last he was aware, I had gone to my eternal rest.

But now comes a gentle roll of laughter, so familiar that my heart nearly bursts to hear it. Trembling, I remove my hands from the table, but I am still afraid to turn.

"Much as I enjoy this particular view of thee, love, I would quite prefer . . ."

I rush to him and crush his lips with mine, capturing the words he's yet to speak. I kiss his cheeks, his eyes, his hair, then draw back to look at him. Our next words come in unison:

"I thought you were dead!"

Our laughter too sounds as one.

"Those months you were gone," I whisper, "you cannot imagine my grief."

"I can imagine well," he assures me. "I was at your funeral!"

"'Tis true, you were at that." My brow wrinkles in confusion. "And yet, upon your waking, you knew 'twas I who stood there at the table. Pray, sir, how?"

"'Tis simple. I would recognize your backside anywhere."

My eyes fly open. The breeches!

"Do not look so embarrassed, love. While I cannot begin to guess why you've taken to wearing pants, I must say I do not mind it in the least, for I confess, the sight of you in them is quite enticing. But you will promise me one thing!"

"Anything, my lord."

"You shall wear more customary attire on the day we are wed."

I am aware of nothing now but the blush upon my cheek and the long, sweet, wonderful kiss I share with Hamlet, Prince of Denmark.

ỡ ỡ ỡ

'Tis well after midnight. Hamlet and I have walked to the stream. In the distance, the windows of Elsinore flicker with candlelight. Hamlet is relieved to hear that his mother will be given a place in the court of Fortinbras. He has already dispatched Tuck with a missive, bidding her farewell.

Anne, who shall go to Wittenberg with Horatio, returned briefly to the castle to gather her belongings. She brought the news of Fortinbras's decision along with a golden ring he bid her give to me as a token of his affection. Claudius was given none of the antidote and was left to expire from the poison.

Hamlet and I will as well remove ourselves from Denmark.

"'Tis strange to think we shall never go back," I say in a wistful tone that surprises me.

"Aye," Hamlet agrees. "Which leads me to this, love. Where exactly will we go? To some sweet-scented isle of flowers where we may spend our midsummer nights among fairies?"

I smile. "Well, since you are asking, my lord, I have been pondering precisely this issue from the moment I learned you were alive." I reach down to pick a daisy and twirl it between my fingers. "What think thee of Italy? In particular, the city of Verona."

"Pray, why there?"

I toss off a dainty shrug. "Something I read in my mother's journal. You see, she often corresponded with an apothecary there. His letters lead me to believe our sleeping poison would interest him greatly."

"Verona." Hamlet strokes his chin, considering. "At

Wittenberg I made the acquaintance of an impetuous fellow from that place. His name, as I recall, was Romeo."

"See there?" I say, eagerly. "'Twould be nice to pay him a
visit, would it not?"

Hamlet shrugs, nods.

"The cost of our voyage is no concern," I remind him,
"since Laertes has offered us the beauteous pearl which
Claudius used to taint the wine. Father says it is a most
costly gem."

"Verona," repeats Hamlet, and now a grin kicks up one
corner of his mouth. "Ah, you know me, love. I cannot
decide."

"Aye, my lord," I say. "But I can." I reach for his hand,
and the journey begins.